Two Kinds of Elizabeth

GENEVIEVE FORTIN

BELLA
BOOKS

2016

Bella Books, Inc.
P.O. Box 10543
Tallahassee, FL 32302

Printed in the United States of America on acid-free paper.

First Bella Books Edition 2016

Editor: Medora MacDougall
Cover Designer: Sandy Knowles

ISBN: 978-1-59493-523-7

Other Bella Books by Genevieve Fortin

First Fall

Acknowledgment

Two Kinds of Elizabeth is a story that sneaked up on me. I'd planned on writing something else as my second novel, but this story wouldn't be ignored. Writing it was a very emotional process for me and so different from my first novel that I was scared to put it out there. I'm still scared in some ways but decided that CC, Liz and Beth all needed to be known more than I needed to feel safe as a writer. I could say more but don't want to give away too much, so all I'll say is that some characters might not get their happy ending in this book, but I will definitely catch up with them in the future. Stay tuned.

I'd like to thank my partner Denise, who loved the story so much that she played a big part in my decision to put my fear aside and publish this novel. I'd also like to thank Medora MacDougall, my wonderful editor. I learned from you and I know I still have a lot to learn from you so I sincerely hope we get to work together again on future books. Thanks to everyone at Bella Books for your support.

And again thank YOU, dear readers, for picking up my book.

Dedication

To all Liz's and those who love them.

About the Author

Genevieve is French Canadian but claims her heart holds dual citizenship. Not surprising since she lived in the USA for thirteen years and still visits every chance she gets. Besides writing and reading, her passions include traveling, decadent desserts, fruity martinis and watching HGTV. For now she lives in St-Georges, just a few miles north of the border between Maine and Quebec. She and her partner share a house with their two dogs, Spike and Betty.

CHAPTER ONE

"Just sayin', CC, for real, everybody knows if you want to keep a secret you don't go telling me nothing right?" Kayla declared as she passed the blunt from the passenger's seat of CC's 1998 Volkswagen Jetta.

CC looked around to make sure she didn't spot a police car before she took a quick hit from the marijuana cigar as she merged onto I-87 South. She gave it back to Kayla before agreeing with her self-assessment. "Right, I never tell you anything unless I don't care if everyone in the office knows about whatever I'm telling you. I learned my lesson when I realized everyone and their mother knew I smoke weed barely a week after you started riding to work with me. I was sure I'd get fired." Kayla didn't drive. When she'd transferred to the Quality Assurance Department, where they worked together, she'd wasted no time asking to ride with CC every morning. Her boyfriend picked her up after work. CC lived in Cohoes, New York, and Kayla was right across the Hudson River in Troy so it was barely a detour on their way to Albany, as long as there was no traffic.

Kayla snickered in that slow, deep and slightly evil way only she could. "Exactly. If that bitch didn't want everyone to know she's sleeping around like a common whore, she should've kept her fucking mouth shut. Just sayin'." CC couldn't help but laugh, almost admiring Kayla's unrepentant attitude. Kayla Munoz was an unapologetic force of nature. She was funny, witty and smart, especially street smart, something CC was definitely not. She was also gorgeous; she had long curly hair and eyes so dark they almost looked black. Yes, she was slightly overweight, and yes, her personality was decidedly abrasive, but she owned her shortcomings with such pride and assertiveness that CC was compelled to like her. And liking Kayla was even easier since CC'd learned that she could not, under any circumstances, trust her to keep a secret. She had a good heart but a big mouth, another trait she refused to apologize for. Kayla's motto was "take me as I am or fuck off," and as long as you accepted that, you could have a wonderful time in her company.

It had taken CC only one week to understand and accept Kayla for who she could be to her: a great coworker and hilarious passenger who contributed to making going to work something she was looking forward to rather than dreading every morning. She worshiped Kayla's confidence. The woman seemed to be known and respected by everyone in the office. Much more discreet and timid, CC talked to only a handful of people daily, and although she'd been working for Dixon & Brown Communications for three years, two years longer than Kayla, she wasn't convinced everyone knew her name yet.

She also envied Kayla's pride in her figure. She hated her own curves so much she did all she could to disappear, hiding under baggy clothes and behind the safe walls of her cubicle all day long. She hadn't gone on a date since her breakup with Michelle, and that was over a year ago. "Pathetic" was the term she most often used to describe herself these days.

She took their exit ramp and turned right onto Wolf Road, glancing at Kayla who swiftly put the blunt away before they pulled into the parking lot of the office building to make sure no one would catch them. The car's clock displayed seven twenty-five a.m. They were five minutes early and her Jetta was the first car there. Even Beth Andrews, their boss and head of the QA department, hadn't yet arrived. Fortunately Beth had convinced management to trust CC with keys to the building, pleading that CC was such a dedicated employee that she would come in during the weekend if she had access to the building, even though CC had done so only twice in her two years in QA to meet tight deadlines.

CC unlocked the one-story brick building and opened the heavy glass door, holding it politely for Kayla. She watched Kayla's long nails, decorated with colorful patterns, as she took one last puff of the cigarette she'd attempted to smoke in the twenty feet that separated the Jetta from the building door. CC coughed when Kayla exhaled and most of the smoke ended up in her face. At last Kayla threw half the cigarette into a large ashtray set by the door for that very purpose and walked in front of CC with a half grin that was meant as a thank you.

CC followed Kayla through a large room crowded with over sixty cubicles. They were empty now, but by eight thirty most of them would be filled with "account representatives," aka telemarketers. The distinguished people of Dixon & Brown Communications who occupied the few closed offices set against the right wall of the building frowned upon the term "telemarketing." In CC's opinion, no matter what you called it, it was still a shitty job. She'd been about to quit after a year of doing it. Fortunately her supervisor had sensed they were going to lose her, and they'd transferred her to the QA department.

They reached the back of the room and Kayla used her own key to unlock a much smaller room, outfitted with only three cubicles: theirs and Beth's. Kayla sat at her own desk and immediately put on her headphones. CC did the same. They would not talk to each other for a little while, focusing on their work and enjoying their morning buzz. Work consisted of listening to recordings of phone conversations between telemarketers and their contacts/victims before determining whether these recordings would be sent as leads—potential sales opportunities—to their clients. The QA team had to make sure the conversation met the client's criteria and expectations. A lead for their largest client, for example, consisted of a business that planned on evaluating accounting software in the next twelve months and had a budget in mind that would cover the approximate cost of the software their client sold. If the lead did not qualify, the QA representatives rejected it. If it qualified, they corrected the disastrous spelling and grammar of the lead notes and sent the lead to the client.

CC loved her job, even though some would say it was just as shitty as being on the phone. Every telemarketer had a lead disqualified at one point or another and some blamed the QA rep for it. Their resentment could be shocking at times. The fact that Kayla had found a way to remain so popular when she became a QA rep was only one more reason CC admired her. No one messed with Kayla.

Another aspect of the job most people disliked was its secluded nature, but CC enjoyed the peace and quiet. Much more social, Kayla took smoke breaks regularly and had even been written up for taking too many, but CC appreciated the isolation and only stepped away from her desk for lunch and rare bathroom breaks. She even liked her cubicle. Slightly larger than the cubicles in the main room, it was surrounded with blue walls that were taller than the usual cubicle walls so it almost felt like a closed office. There was no door, of course, but at least there was a skylight in the high ceiling of the room that compensated for the absence of windows. She was comfortable in her cubicle. Work wasn't a burden for CC. It was her haven.

"Good morning," Beth announced as she entered the QA room.

"Good morning," CC and Kayla answered in unison. CC heard Beth set down her keys and purse in the largest of the three cubicles, and she salivated when she heard the familiar crinkling of a paper bag.

"Help yourselves to some bagels, ladies. Happy Friday!"

"For real, you're the coolest boss ever," Kayla said. She grabbed a bagel and disappeared after stating she was going to toast her breakfast in the breakroom. CC knew Kayla would also jump on the opportunity for a first smoke break. They'd been working for fifteen minutes.

"Thank you so much Beth. You know you don't have to do this for us every Friday right? You're spoiling us," CC said as she approached Beth's desk and the bag of bagels. Beth smiled tenderly and closed both of her eyes for a long moment before opening them again, something she did often. CC never could decide if the gesture was a very strange two-eye-wink or merely a weird eyelid-nod, but she had learned to recognize it as a sign of acknowledgment and an expression of Beth's pure kindness.

"I know, but I love doing it. My team is very small, but I like to show how much I appreciate you. There's one with sesame seeds for you." CC smiled and reached into the bag for the sesame bagel before taking one of the plastic knifes and a small container of cream cheese from Beth's desk. She started walking back to her own cubicle when Beth added, "Don't forget your coffee."

CC took the large Dunkin' Donuts hazelnut coffee with cream that Beth had brought for her. She brought one every morning. She'd started when it was only the two of them in the department and continued to do so even when Kayla joined them. CC was certain Kayla'd noticed, but she didn't seem to mind the flagrant preferential treatment that flattered CC. "Thank you," she said.

"You're most welcome, Ciel," Beth answered.

Ciel Charbonneau did not particularly dislike her name, but people had started calling her CC in Cohoes High School, and she'd let them. It was much easier than explaining how her name was pronounced "See-Elle," not "Seal" or "Shell," and how it meant "sky" in French. She'd learned that the explanation inevitably led to another long story about her parents' obsession with their French-Canadian origins and the peace and love movement they'd embraced even though at barely ten years of age they had been too young to attend Woodstock, a tragedy that still brought tears to their eyes every time they mentioned it. Beth was the only person besides her parents who called her Ciel, stating her name was too beautiful not to be said and heard as often as possible. CC didn't mind it at all.

CHAPTER TWO

Like most Friday nights, CC was getting ready to celebrate the end of the workweek by herself in her one-bedroom loft. She'd already changed into yoga pants and a vintage T-shirt, and a thin crust pizza from a small Italian place in South Troy was keeping warm in the oven. Although she smoked blunts with Kayla, she preferred a regular joint, and she was about to light up, sitting on the cozy built-in window seat tucked in the alcove of an open eight-foot tall window of her living room. She was letting the June breeze caress her face for a minute when she heard the distinctive and annoying sound of the intercom. She set the joint on the window seat with a grunt and went to answer, knowing it could only be her parents.

"Hey, guys, come on up." She opened the door for them and got three wine glasses out of the kitchen cupboards, knowing her parents would bring a bottle. They joined her one or two Fridays a month to celebrate the weekend. CC suspected they always hoped they'd surprise her with a date or, better yet, that there would be no answer because CC would be out somewhere—as any twenty-nine-year-old single woman should be on a Friday night. But they never let their disappointment show when they found her home alone.

"Knock knock," her mother said uselessly as she entered the loft. "God, I can't get over how nice this place is. You can smell the history." Marie Charbonneau looked up to the fourteen-feet-high ceiling and down to the original hardwood floors in awe as she always did. CC often thought the proudest she'd made her parents was when she moved to her loft. It was modern and looked as beautiful as something you would see in a magazine, which compensated for its small square footage, but what mattered most to her parents what that it was located in a converted 1870s cotton mill, a place where their French-Canadian ancestors had left their hearts and sweat as millworkers.

"Yes, it sure was a smart investment," Charles Charbonneau added, hugging his daughter. She'd bought the loft after inheriting from her paternal grandfather. His success had been vaguely attributed to business and real estate and she'd always imagined it was not entirely legal, but the money he'd left her had allowed her to make a down payment large enough to be able to afford the mortgage on her own place. CC agreed that it had been a very smart move, especially since she would never be able to afford a home on her salary as a QA rep.

"So, how are you guys? Tough week?" She hugged her mother and took the bottle of Sauvignon Blanc from her dad's hands before going back to the open concept kitchen to open it.

"Yes, you could say that. George had another psychotic episode and refuses to take his medication. He had to be hospitalized again. I'm getting too old for that crap." Marie ended her sentence with a heavy sigh and, as if catching herself, smiled and waved her hand in front of her face in a dismissive gesture. "But enough about me. How was your week, honey?"

"Oh, same shit, different week. Nothing to report. I worry about you, Mom. It seems it's getting harder for you to leave work at work."

"I tell her that every day, baby," Charles added in support.

"Oh, would you stop, you two? What am I supposed to do? I can't retire at fifty-five, can I?"

"Why not? The house is paid for. We wouldn't live rich, but we could manage," Charles argued. Marie gave him a tender kiss on the lips, as much to shut him up as to thank him, CC thought. CC looked at the tall, slim man in front of her and smiled at his clear, kind blue eyes and his grey mustache. Her dad was a good man. He worked as a French teacher at Cohoes High and never made much money, but she knew he meant every word he said. He couldn't bear the stress his wife was under and would do all he could to convince her to retire early. Marie worked as a social worker for the community counseling center. Her work as a case manager focused on the social rehabilitation of patients suffering from severe mental illness. It had always weighed heavily on her emotionally, but it had become worse in the past few months. CC stared at the beautiful woman standing in her kitchen, the only wrinkles on her face taking shape in subtle crow's feet on the side of each deep, almost navy blue eye, and vowed to help her dad convince her to retire before stress did more damage.

"He's right, mom. You could manage perfectly well on one salary at this stage of your life."

"Maybe, honey, but how can I abandon them?" And there was the real issue. Marie's mind would be easy to convince, but her heart was another story. She loved her patients. Each and every one of them. Even George, the biggest pain in her ass.

"You wouldn't be abandoning them, Mom. Someone else would take over. Who knows, maybe that's what they need. Aren't you the one who told me patients can only grow so much with the same person and change can help them grow further?" CC handed a glass of wine to each of her parents before taking her own.

"I know, I know. Okay, I'll think about it. Now could we get off this topic, please? I propose a toast to our beautiful daughter," Marie said raising her glass. CC winced at the word "beautiful" and Marie lowered her glass. "No, no, no, none of that, young lady. Come on, Ciel! Have you looked at yourself in a mirror lately? That hair, those eyes, those curves. You're gorgeous, honey. When will you start believing that?"

"I second that," Charles added, raising his own glass. CC did like her eyes, always blue but going from the light sky blue of her father's eyes to the dark blue of her mother's depending on her mood, the weather or the color of her clothes. She also liked the thick wavy brown hair that flowed freely to just below her shoulders. But the curves, the curves she could not accept. "Curvy" was just another word for "fat." She hated her fat. She smiled anyway and raised her own glass.

"I really wish I could see myself the way you see me. Here's to trying harder." They clinked their glasses together, and they each took a sip. "Oh that's good," CC said. "You know what would go well with this?" she asked with a wink, motioning for her parents to follow her to the window. They laughed when she showed them the joint.

"We raised you well, kid," her dad declared when she handed him the joint and a lighter. Her mother's laughing eyes agreed with a wink. Her parents had stopped hiding their smoking habit when they caught her smoking her own stash in her bedroom as a teenager. They started sharing a smoke once in a while, but never on a school night.

At first CC was conflicted about it all, knowing perfectly well her parents were not the usual parents. Like any teenager she hesitated to embrace her parents' uniqueness, wanting nothing more than to blend in. Being raised by hippy-wannabes was not something she wished for. As an adult, however, she was grateful for her parents' easygoing nature and most of all their boundless kindness and generosity.

"And you're staying for pizza. I have way too much for myself," CC declared when her mother handed her the joint.

"Ooh, Carlotta's?" Marie asked between her clenched teeth, trying to hold the marijuana smoke as long as she could.

"You know it, Mom."

"Excellent! I love you, honey."

"I love you too, guys."

CHAPTER THREE

"Ciel, could you please handle the training for the new AccBreezy campaign at nine a.m.? They double-booked me again and since you're the main QA rep on the AccBreezy account I was hoping you could take this one. I'll take the event boost training." Beth was standing by CC's desk with a hesitant yet hopeful expression.

As the head of the QA department, Beth was expected to attend all new campaign trainings so she could share the guidelines with her team afterward. The main reason management had made Beth's presence at all new trainings mandatory, however, was so she could ask the client relationship manager pointed questions that clarified how strict those guidelines were for all account representatives as well as the supervisor who attended the training. They hoped this would limit the disqualification rate. And it did, to a certain extent. CC had to admit that, but it didn't stop her from hating the fact that Beth was getting double-booked more and more often, especially on Monday mornings like today when more than one new campaign was about to be launched. That meant she had to attend trainings too. She hated having to play the devil's advocate and ask those uncomfortable questions that would, all hoped, leave no doubt in everyone's mind what was going to be accepted and what was going to be rejected. She felt like she had to be cold, almost mean, to be taken seriously in those trainings, and that was not her at all. Friendly, sweet, timid CC didn't do mean. But that was not Beth's fault. And it did make sense for her to attend the training since she would be the QA rep responsible for the campaign. So she looked up to Beth and smiled, "No problem, I'll be there."

The grateful smile on Beth's face appeased some of the anxiety that had already started suffocating CC. "Thank you, Ciel. I knew I could count on you. Let me know if you need help, but I'm sure you already know what to ask right?"

"Of course, boss. You trained me well." Beth blinked slowly as CC expected she would to acknowledge her comment and smiled again before going back to her own desk. CC was left wondering, not for the first time, how such an amiable woman could appear to be so comfortable with the reputation of being a cold-hearted bitch that she'd earned as head of QA. Her heart warmed up briefly, as she savored the privilege of being allowed to witness the gentle nature behind the reputation. And then the suffocating anxiety took over again.

Time to let my own inner bitch loose, she thought. *Wake up, bitch*.

* * *

An hour later CC was sitting at the rectangular table of the large conference room with pen and notepad. The new AccBreezy campaign was going to be much larger than the new event boost so Beth and a handful of account reps were probably crowding a client relationship manager's office right now while CC was focusing on her breathing, sitting around the table with a dozen account reps and Lindsey Barrett, one of the supervisors. CC looked around the room as they waited for the client relationship manager to join them. Her gaze first locked on Lindsey, a bubbly and sharp-minded cheerleader type in her midtwenties. CC thought she was a great supervisor and had appreciated working on her team when she first started at Dixon & Brown Communications. She returned Lindsey's smile before studying other faces around the large table. Most were the usual suspects and CC's gaze was met with polite nods at best and resentful glares at worst with the occasional "I can't even look at you so I'll pretend I'm reading this stupid script right now" vibe.

She was surprised when she reached the spot directly across from her at the table and was met with a genuine smile. New girl, obviously. The smile reached piercing green eyes and CC was forced to smile back. Her mouth went dry. She could no longer be sure if it was due to her nerves or to the striking beauty facing her. Long red hair, beautiful ivory skin, a subtle and sexy cleft in her chin and those eyes that kept CC staring. The spell was broken when Jeff finally entered the room and took his spot at the end of the table.

Jeff Hudson was an asshole and as dumb as a rock, if you asked CC. She couldn't understand how he'd kept his job for the past three years. He'd sent through several so-called opportunities to his clients, even though CC had rejected them because they didn't qualify, only to make his quota. She'd never argued with him about it because managers had the power to overturn the decision of a QA rep at any time so ultimately it was out of her hands, but she found his lack of ethics infuriating. He seemed to be lacking ethics in all aspects of his life. About the same age as CC, Jeff looked good and could be charming as hell. And he knew it. Many girls from the office had fallen for him, and if you believed the rumors that were too frequent and abundant not to be at least partially true, he didn't let the fact that he had a fiancée stop him from an easy conquest once in a while. He was disgusting.

CC didn't hate men, far from it. Her dad had always been a great role model and she'd had close male friends in her school years. She knew there were as many great men as there were great women out there, even if she didn't want to sleep with them. Yet she was certain if Jeff had been the first man she'd encountered in her life she would have jumped on the man-hating wagon, if there was such a thing. She hated the guy, plain and simple, and had no respect for him whatsoever. And she knew he didn't like her either. Probably because she saw through his bullshit, she thought.

"I see you all have the script. Great, thanks for that Lindsey," Jeff said with a wink to Lindsey. *Puke.* He then directed his gaze to drop-dead-gorgeous new girl and continued, "And I think you wanted to introduce someone before we get started with the training?" He grinned at the beautiful redhead before turning back to Lindsey. *Double puke.*

"Yes, thank you, Jeff," Lindsey started, getting everyone's attention. "You've probably all noticed we have a new face in the room. I'd like you all to join me in welcoming Elizabeth McLeary. Elizabeth is a business student at U Albany and she's here with us for the summer. Welcome to the D&B family, Elizabeth."

Everyone clapped with as much enthusiasm as they could muster on a Monday morning, which was not much at all. CC became aware of her contrasting ardor—she was clapping and smiling gleefully—and attempted to rein in her joy, but Elizabeth had already noticed, winking at her in a way that left her cheeks warm with the blush of instant infatuation, a feeling that was as embarrassing as unexpected, yet not unpleasant.

Elizabeth also blushed from the attention and addressed the entire room when she said, "Thanks everyone. Please call me Liz."

"You got it, Liz," Jeff said with another of his vile winks before bringing everyone's attention to the training. CC missed the first ten minutes of his blah-blah-blah because she was too busy watching Liz as discretely as humanly possible. She was quite proud of her technique until Liz, without ever taking her eyes or attention away from Jeff's presentation, turned her notepad toward CC long enough for her to read the four words she'd quickly scribbled: "You are so adorable."

CC felt unbearable heat creep up her chest and cheeks and didn't look at Liz again, focusing her full attention to Jeff's rubbish. He'd finished going over the script and it was her inner bitch's turn to speak. "Jeff, if I may, I'd like to clarify a few things so we're all on the same page."

It seemed to hurt him, but he still nodded and said, "Go ahead, CC."

"The third question in the script asks if the company plans on purchasing accounting software in the next twelve months. That's different from the usual script that simply asks if they're evaluating software. That makes me think I should disqualify leads where contacts just plan on evaluating, am I right?"

He hesitated, looking at her like she spoke a foreign language. "I don't think that makes a difference, does it, CC? It's the same thing."

"Well, not really, Jeff." She took a condescending tone and was surprised in the pleasure she found in it. "A company could be *evaluating* software within the next twelve months even though they do not plan on *purchasing* anything for the next two years or so. We all know the buying cycle for this type of software can take a really long time and it seems to me that if the client used the word *purchasing*, it's because they want a company that is really planning on *purchasing* within twelve months, not just *evaluating*. Big difference. I mean, I could go to every open house in town *evaluating* houses without planning on *purchasing* anything at all right?" A few people chuckled, including Liz, but CC kept her eyes on Jeff, who shifted positions uncomfortably in his seat.

"Right, you've got a point, CC. I'll check with the client and I'll get back to you and Lindsey."

"Thank you, Jeff," she said with a plastic smile. Jeff resumed talking, summarizing the benefits of the software their client expected account reps to list during their calls. CC knew them all already, but she kept a serious expression, taking copious notes as if she was really interested in what he said. No one else knew most of her notes actually read "Jeff Hudson, you're an idiot" over and over again.

Suddenly she was aware of eyes on her. Green, penetrating eyes from across the table. It took all she had to keep another blush from betraying her, but in the end she was able to maintain her fake intense focus on Jeff. She turned to a new page on her notepad and wrote a question. Without taking her eyes off Jeff, she subtly turned the pad sideways, knowing Liz would read: "Still adorable?"

Jeff finally shut his mouth and the training was over. Everyone stood up and CC dared a quick glance at Liz, who smiled at her and lowered her eyes to her own notepad, inviting CC to read: "Yes, and oh so sexy." She swallowed hard as Liz left the room with everyone else. She remained behind, powerless to move.

"If I'd known you could be sexy, bitch, I would've let you out a long time ago," she muttered to her inner bitch.

CHAPTER FOUR

"Word is you put that fucktard in his place, CC. You're hard core. I'm so proud of you," Kayla said with her signature snicker as they entered the QA room the next morning. CC elbowed Kayla, silently begging her to shut up; Beth was already sitting at her desk. Fortunately Beth didn't ask any questions about Kayla's comment. But of course she would not. Beth never showed any interest in Kayla's or anyone else's gossip. CC only hoped Jeff or even Lindsey hadn't complained about her. She'd spent the night in paranoid mode, worried that her attitude might have been seen as disrespectful. Jeff Hudson, as moronic as he was, was still a member of the management team after all.

"Good morning, ladies," Beth simply said.

"Morning boss," Kayla replied before sitting at her desk.

CC offered the same polite greeting, sat in her cubicle and put on her headphones. She was too busy being paranoid, a state of mind certainly heightened by her morning buzz, to notice there was no coffee waiting for her on her desk. Beth typically left the large Styrofoam cup filled with warm heaven in front of her computer screen when she came in before CC. When Beth appeared in CC's cubicle with the missing coffee in hand, CC realized it had indeed been sorely missing from her life. She grabbed the cup with both hands. "Oh thank you, you're too good to me," she said sincerely.

Beth leaned against CC's desk. "You're most welcome. I wanted to let you know I forwarded you an email from Jeff. He was following up on a question you asked during yesterday's training. The client wants reps to make sure leads are generated with companies that plan on purchasing within twelve months, not just evaluating. Apparently they tightened up that question on purpose because they thought 'evaluating' was too vague and they didn't like the leads it generated for them in the previous campaigns. Excellent work, Ciel. Thanks for asking that question. I knew I could count on you."

"I was only doing my job."

"I know. But you made sure someone else was forced to do his too. That's the real accomplishment here." She offered her warmest smile and winked at CC, a genuine, one-eye, understanding wink that made CC proud and erased all traces of paranoia. She'd done the right thing and Beth was backing her up. One hundred percent. She smiled at Beth and watched her leave her cubicle as she took her first sip of creamy hazelnut delight.

* * *

CC had not seen Liz again since the training, and she felt her cheeks heat up instantly when she literally bumped into her on her way to the restroom during mid-morning break. She was looking down to the floor as she walked quickly past the breakroom and didn't notice when the door opened and Liz came out. Her hip bumped into her firm buttocks before she could stop. "Oh hi," she said weakly when she met the green eyes. "Sorry, I didn't see you."

Liz was now facing her and a mocking smile was on her full lips. "Oh damn. And here I was thinking you were trying to grab my ass. News flash: no need to fake-bump into me next time." CC felt her face turn a darker shade of red, but thankfully Liz grinned and continued before she was forced to answer. "On your way to the restroom?" CC nodded. "Great, I was on my way there too. Mind if I join you?"

"I'm pretty sure it's a public restroom," CC managed, satisfied with the girly laugh that easily came out of Liz's mouth.

They started walking side by side, and Liz casually grabbed the hem of the white and blue peasant blouse that fell loosely over CC's jeans. "I love the look. Very cool. And the blue accents really make your eyes pop."

"Thank you," CC answered, embarrassed by the compliment. "It's not as stylish as your outfit, but it's comfy." They reached the restroom, and CC pushed the door open and leaned her back against it, keeping it open for Liz. Liz started walking past her slowly, closer than needed. CC sucked in her stomach, trying to disappear when she felt round breasts barely brush against hers. Liz stopped for a brief moment, her face inches from CC's.

"Stylish, huh? Why, thank you, Ms. Charbonneau. I didn't think you noticed." The words were almost whispered, and CC held her breath until Liz continued into the room. She couldn't help taking another look at the overall picture that Liz presented, even though she was very aware that Liz could follow her gaze in the large mirror they were now facing. High heels, black pencil skirt showcasing lean and athletic legs, tight emerald sweater highlighting every deliciously feminine curve and luxurious red hair put up into a casual bun with tempting tendrils falling on each side of a beautiful face covered with subtle makeup. "Stylish" was the most polite word CC could use to describe the portrait. She ended her inspection when she met Liz's eyes in the mirror. They took the same emerald green of her sweater, and their intense glare gave CC a high that made her uncharacteristically brave.

"I most certainly noticed, Ms. McLeary," she said in a voice so low and husky that it surprised her. She didn't mean to be so obvious and she suddenly felt embarrassed, so she joined Liz at the sinks and started washing her hands, imitating the redhead. "So, you study business?"

"Yes, first year at U Albany." At CC's puzzled look Liz chuckled and continued, "Don't worry, I'm not that young. I'm twenty-four. I tried a few things before I settled on business. If I change majors again, I think my parents might very well kill me. No kidding."

They laughed and when Liz opened the door to exit the restroom, CC followed, ignoring a bladder that so desperately needed to evacuate the large coffee consumed earlier. They walked slowly side by side and kept chatting. "So you're a professional student," CC said with a teasing grin. "Interesting. What else have you tried, if I may ask? And why business in the end?"

"Oh god, I started in arts. Painting. Then art history because I thought it would make me a better artist. Then early education because I thought I'd like to teach art to little kids. And then last year I tried some psychology classes, I guess because I was trying to understand myself more than anything else. And why business? Because I finally realized my parents were right and there's no money to be made in anything else I tried, and as my dad says," she made her voice deeper and furrowed her eyebrows to impersonate her father, "'It's about damn time you get serious and get a real career, pumpkin. College is not cheap and you're not getting any younger.'"

Liz finished with a smile that appeared so sad to CC. Regretting the fact that they'd already arrived at Liz's cubicle, she decided to linger for a minute. "Do you still paint?" she asked.

"Yes. It's more like a hobby now, but I can't stop."

CC was pleased to see the green eyes light up again and relieved Liz's parents had not completely killed her passion yet. "Great. I'd like to see what you paint some time."

"Really?"

Liz's expression was both endearing and heartbreaking, as if anyone showing interest in her art was completely shocking, almost inconceivable. "Yes, really. I admire artistic people."

Realizing other account reps were now noticing her presence on the floor and looking at her like a rare animal escaped from the zoo, CC took Liz's pen and wrote her cell phone number on her notepad. "Call me anytime." Before Liz could answer she walked to the back of the room and disappeared into the cage that was the QA room. She was taken aback by how bold she'd just been. She'd never before given her phone number to a woman without being asked, but she was so drawn to Liz she simply couldn't help it. Everything about her screamed that she was worth the risk.

CHAPTER FIVE

Thursday evening CC made her way to the neighborhood of Troy where Kayla lived with her boyfriend, Damon. Although she stopped in front of Kayla's door every morning to pick her up without giving any thought to her surroundings, things were quite different in the evening. Especially in the summer. The streets were full of up-to-no-good kids and it seemed there was a police car at every corner. Of course, her impression might have been heightened by the fact that this trip was her weekly replenishment mission; she bought her weed from Damon every Thursday evening. She parallel parked her Jetta between an Escalade SUV and a semi pimped-out Dodge Stratus and made her way to a Victorian house that had been divided into apartments, looking as cool and aloof as she could so she wouldn't raise suspicion.

Damon opened the door before she could ring the bell and motioned her inside. She greeted him with a hug and a quick kiss on the cheek and walked into the cloud of marijuana smoke. Without waiting for further invitation she took a seat on the dark brown sectional that occupied three walls of the small living room. Damon didn't want anyone to simply go in and out of their place, making the purpose of their visit obvious to any cop keeping watch on the neighborhood. So CC made a habit of staying for an hour or so, chatting with her friends before leaving with her stash. She enjoyed their visits very much. Sadly they were often the most social event of her week.

Damon sat down next to Kayla, wrapping his arm around her shoulders. He was tall, dark, and could definitely look intimidating if you didn't know him. To CC, however, he was nothing but a sweet teddy bear, and she thought he and Kayla made a great couple. They'd been together for five years.

"So what's the latest D&B news? Did I miss anything this week?" she asked Kayla as she sat farther back into her seat and made herself comfortable, knowing that little bit of prompting was enough to get Kayla talking for most of her visit.

"Well, did I tell you about Joanna blowing Jeff in her Beamer in front of Applebee's?"

"What?"

"That's what Jimmy told me." At CC's blank stare Kayla added, "Cute blond gay boy from Hayley's team? Worst lead notes ever because he can't spell for shit?" Hayley was the other account supervisor at Dixon & Brown, and Jimmy was indeed cute and tragically bad at spelling and grammar. CC finally nodded with recognition and Kayla continued, "Well, he works at Applebee's nights and weekends as a waiter and he saw them Tuesday night. Getting nasty in that bright red convertible right in front of the restaurant. Now I'm not surprised about Jeff. We all know that fucker's trash. But Joanna? I thought that bitch had class, just sayin'."

"Wait a minute; you're talking about *the* Joanna right?"

"The one and only Joanna Dixon, co-founder of Dixon & Brown Communications."

Kayla took the blunt Damon handed her as CC let the words sink in. She finally shook her head. "No way. I don't believe any of it. That woman is way too smart for dumb-fuck Jeff Hudson. And she's married to an attractive, successful man. No way.

Obviously Jimmy misunderstood something. Maybe they were getting ready to leave after a business dinner and she dropped a file in the car. When she picked it up it could've looked like she was...you know. But no, there's no way she actually did that. No way."

"Whoa, CC, why so defensive? Do you have a crush on boss-lady?"

"No but I respect her, almost admire her. And imagining her with that asshole ruins that for me. So please, don't mention it again. It's totally gross."

"Okay, okay, don't get your panties in a twist. I'm just the messenger here but I won't mention the Double J Triple X incident again. Moving on to the second top gossip of the week. And I must say, CC, I'm a little hurt you said nothing to me about this one. I thought I was your friend."

"What? What is it? You're freaking me out here. Is it about me?"

Kayla's eyes became two tiny glassy slits as she snickered before she answered. "Oh yes. About you and fire-crotch-newbie doing the nasty in the restroom. Damn, girl, I didn't know you had it in you."

"For real? You go, CC. That's my girl," Damon added, obviously amused. CC's cheeks were on fire, and she had to jump off the sectional and pace frantically to let the steam out.

"See? That's complete bullshit. Damn it, you can't believe anything you hear in that place! Liz and I happened to go in and out of the restroom at the same time, but we just washed our hands, for Christ's sake. That's all. People really think we did it in there?"

"Yep. People sure do. But come on, CC, can you blame them? The two of you write cute little notes, make goo-goo eyes at each other all week long and on top of that you disappear behind closed doors together. People jump to conclusions real easy in that office. You should know that."

"What? How the hell do you know about the notes? And goo-goo eyes? Come on!"

"Look, all I'm saying is people know you're queer and fire-crotch goes around telling anyone who'll listen she's bi. Then the two of you get a little cozy, and don't you fucking deny it. Mix all that in the rumor mill and you get scandalous lesbian loving in the restroom. Simple as that."

"Well, in case you have any interest in the truth, there was none of that. A couple of notes, yes. Maybe a few looks. But that's it. No scandalous lesbian loving anywhere. I didn't even know she was bi. Is she really?"

"That's what she says. That and that you have such pretty blue eyes. Gag me." Kayla rolled her eyes dramatically.

"She said that?" CC asked more calmly as she sat back down.

"She did," Kayla repeated.

"Sounds like CC's gonna get some pussy," Damon said enthusiastically, gently patting Kayla's thigh.

"It's about damn time if you ask me," Kayla added.

"Oh shut up, you two. And please, K, please don't ever call her fire-crotch again. It's tacky."

Kayla and Damon laughed like a pair of co-conspirators before Kayla gave in. "All right, I won't. Not until you confirm she's a real redhead anyway." She winked at Damon and the two of them laughed harder, clearly finding CC's emerging love life hilarious. CC couldn't find it in her to be as offended as she thought she should be, because she was already too busy being torn between her prudent disbelief and gleeful excitement at the thought of having a love life at all.

* * *

That night CC couldn't find sleep. She tossed and turned in her bed until eleven and then finally chose to get up. She sat in the window seat of her living room, her preferred spot to read. She decided against the lesbian romance novel she'd recently purchased and went for Hillary Rodham Clinton's *Hard Choices*. She figured reading about her favorite political figure's experience as secretary of state would help her get Liz out of her mind while the steamy erotic scenes described by

Gerri Hill would only make things worse. She was right; an hour later she was finally dozing off so she went back to bed.

When she heard a beeping sound, she painfully opened her eyes and looked at her alarm clock; she'd been sleeping for less than an hour. She grunted into her pillow. She heard the beeping sound again and recognized the sound as notification of an incoming text message on her cell phone. "What the hell?" she cried to herself.

A sudden panic took over then. Nothing short of an emergency would lead someone to text her so late at night. In the time it took her to jump out of bed and run to the small device sitting on the living room coffee table, she had time to imagine both of her parents dying of a heart attack, a stroke and a violent car accident. Her heart was racing uncontrollably when she finally looked at the display screen and saw that the text came from a number she didn't know and simply read, "Hi."

Too angry to ignore the intruder, she texted back, "It's the middle of the night, moron, so fuck off!" She tossed the phone back onto the coffee table but didn't have time to walk all the way back to the bedroom before another text chimed in. She sighed heavily but went back to the phone to read what the intruder had to say.

"Sorry CC. It's me, Liz."

CC furrowed her brows and slumped onto the couch to type her answer.

"Oh. Hi. It's okay. Sorry I yelled at you. Is something wrong?"

"Yeah."

"Anything I can help with?"

"Maybe. You can tell me you don't think I'm a loser."

CC texted as quickly as she could, running their conversations over and over in her mind as she typed with both thumbs and unable to find any reason why Liz would have such worries. "I don't understand. Why would I think you're a loser?" She waited for the answer for what seemed like an eternity, nervously tapping her thigh with her hand.

"Because I'm twenty-four and don't have a degree yet. Because I can't make up my mind about what I want to do with my life. Because I had a zit on my chin when you looked at me in the restroom mirror."

CC brought one knee to her chest and leaned her chin on it for a minute, thinking of her answer. She didn't expect such insecurity from Liz and she didn't know how to respond. Her vulnerability didn't make her less attractive however. Quite the opposite. CC found herself wishing the redhead was sitting on her couch right now so she could answer with a warm, comforting embrace instead of words. The words finally came.

"I'm nearly thirty and don't have a degree either. You've already put more thought into what you want to do with your life than I ever did. And believe me all I saw in that mirror is how stunningly beautiful you are." Her heart started beating loudly when she hit "send." More excruciating waiting.

"Thank you, that's sweet. But then why haven't you talked to me since that day?"

CC had stayed locked up in the QA room for the couple of days after she gave Liz her phone number, partly because she'd been so uncharacteristically bold that she was afraid of what she would do next and mostly because she was afraid of rejection. She was the insecure one, after all. The plain, boring, timid one. Liz was the gorgeous, confident bombshell. What the hell was happening now? What kind of alternate universe had she fallen into that she was the one needing to reassure Liz?

"I gave you my phone number, didn't I? You're the one who waited two days to use it." She added a smiley face to make sure Liz would know she meant to tease.

"LOL. I guess you're right. So, if I ask you on a date you might still say yes?"

The goofy grin on CC's face expressed her joy while her sweaty hands betrayed her nerves when she typed. "Ask and you'll see." This time she dared the emoticon version of a wink.

"Would you go out with me tomorrow night?"

"Absolutely."

"Great! See you at work. And I'm so sorry I woke you up."

"I'm not, so don't worry about it. See you tomorrow. Sweet dreams."

"You too, cutie."

CC set her phone back on the coffee table and almost skipped rather than walked back to her bedroom. She brought Hillary Rodham Clinton with her, knowing she would most definitely need the First Lady's help if she was ever going back to sleep.

CHAPTER SIX

On Friday morning CC was floating. She couldn't focus on work, her brain constantly going back to the tentative date Liz had made with her. It was already ten in the morning and her bagel still sat on her desk practically untouched, just like her coffee. Thinking she heard a knock on the door of the QA room, she took off her headphones. No one ever came to the QA room. When CC heard the knock again she went to answer it. She smiled when she saw Liz standing in front of her with a sweet grin on her lovely face.

"Good morning," she said as she stepped closer to CC.

"Good morning."

"Were you able to go back to sleep last night?" Liz played with the top button of CC's oversized, light blue Oxford shirt.

"Yes," CC lied.

"Good." She didn't stop playing with CC's shirt until the top two buttons were open, exposing a hint of cleavage. "There, much better," she assessed with sparkling green eyes.

CC focused on controlling her breathing and suddenly remembered she was still standing at the entry of the QA room. "Listen, you shouldn't be here." At Liz's hurt expression, CC rushed to continue, "I'm really sorry. Reps are not allowed in the QA room. Can we talk at lunch?"

Liz stretched out her neck to see behind CC and asked teasingly, "What's the big deal? What are you ladies hiding back there?"

"May I help you?" The question came from Beth. Although they'd been almost whispering, Beth had heard them and was now standing right behind CC, glaring at Liz.

CC backed away to make room for her boss in the narrow space at the door. Beth was taller than CC by no more than a couple of inches, but she suddenly seemed to tower over her. "Sorry Beth. Liz was just leaving."

Liz refused to acknowledge CC's cue and remained rooted in her spot. "Actually, I had one more question for CC, if you don't mind giving us a moment."

CC sent Liz a look mixed with disbelief and warning, but Liz didn't move. CC could only watch as the two women faced each other in a wordless duel that seemed to last for weeks. Beth was the first one to talk, and when she did her tone was polite but glacial and as ruthless as her reputation.

"I'm sorry, Liz is it?" Liz nodded. "Right. I'm sorry, Liz, but your question will have to wait. No reps are allowed in this room. No exceptions." And just like that, without giving Liz a chance to respond, she closed the door in her adversary's face and turned to CC. "This can't happen again, Ciel. Are we clear on that?"

"Yes, very clear. It won't happen again. I'm sorry."

Beth dropped her gaze to CC's partly unbuttoned shirt. Her cheeks flushed, and she stared into CC's eyes one last time with disappointment and disapproval before turning away and going back to her desk. CC had never before believed Beth's gentle eyes could really be that cold, but in this moment she was chilled to her core and she wanted to cry. She slowly buttoned her shirt as Kayla entered the room with a fresh whiff of cigarette on her clothes.

"What the fuck happened to Carrot-Bitch? She looks like she's ready to murder someone."

"Shh, K. I'll explain later." Kayla understood and accepted CC's plea to drop the subject. She shrugged and sat nonchalantly at her desk. CC stepped closer and mouthed, "Carrot-Bitch?"

"What? CC, you've got to give me something here." She smirked and CC was forced to smile back.

"Fine, I guess that's better than the other thing you called her."

"I knew you'd agree."

* * *

At lunch time CC looked for Liz in the breakroom and saw her sitting with four other reps at one of the larger round tables in the room. She lingered in front of the microwave oven and when Liz didn't come to talk to her as she'd hoped she opted to sit alone at a smaller table by the exit. She'd never felt very comfortable eating in the breakroom; she could still count on one hand the times she'd done so since she started working at D&B. When she saw Liz follow her peers on their way out of the room she felt a lump in her throat. As the redhead walked by her table she gently grabbed her wrist to stop her. "Could we talk for a moment, please?"

Liz seemed to hesitate but finally took the seat across the small table from CC. "I'm sorry about what happened this morning."

"That was very embarrassing, CC. I can't believe you let that woman talk to me that way." She was fuming. CC didn't quite understand why she was so angry but thought trying to explain was probably better than telling Liz she was overreacting.

"I know it must have been very embarrassing, and I'm sorry about that. But that woman is my boss, Liz. And I couldn't go against her and her rules. That's why I was trying to suggest that we should talk at lunch time. I'm really, really sorry if that hurt you." CC covered Liz's hand with hers on the table and watched as the rage left her communicative eyes almost as quickly as it had appeared, only to be replaced by something CC couldn't identify until Liz dropped her head to the table.

"Oh no. God, I'm such an idiot. I got you in trouble, didn't I?

Although CC much preferred Liz's guilt to her rage, she didn't mean to burden her with culpability so she grinned as she held her index and thumb an inch apart. "Just a little," she said lightly, trying her best to keep the still too-recent memory of Beth's icy stare at bay. "It's no big deal, don't worry. I simply had to promise you wouldn't come to the QA room again."

"I won't, I promise. Oh god, CC, I'm so sorry. Are you sure you want to go out with me? We haven't gone out on our first date yet and I already woke you up in the middle of the night and got you in trouble with your boss. I'm nothing but a hassle. I'll understand if you want to cancel."

CC caressed Liz's hand in a slow comforting motion. "Hey now. No one's cancelling. I'm not really in trouble with Beth as long as it doesn't happen again. And I don't mind if you wake me up in the middle of the night. Although I bet it would be more fun if you did it in person." CC felt her own blush as she spoke the words but seeing Liz smile again was worth the slight discomfort.

Liz moved her hand from under CC's and laced their fingers together. Her eyes were now filled with affection and tenderness, and CC melted when she asked softly, "So, we're still on for tonight then?"

"Yes, we're on. What do you want to do?" CC leaned her elbow on the table to support her chin in her free hand, staring into Liz's eyes. They were now alone in the breakroom.

Liz mimicked her position before she answered. "Would it be okay if I brought food to your place? I've been working on a painting I'd really like to show you in private. I'd invite you to my place, but my roommate will be there. You do live alone, don't you?"

CC tried to ignore her pounding heart and answered as smoothly as she could. "I do, and I'd love to have you over. I can't wait to see your painting."

"Great. Do you like Thai?"

"I love Thai."

"Perfect. Text me your address this afternoon. I'll be there around six." They stared into each other's eyes for a few more seconds before CC glanced at the clock on the wall and was abruptly reminded lunch hour had been over for more than five minutes. She reluctantly took her hand away from Liz's.

"Right, I'll text you. See you later."

"See you later, sweetie." As she walked back to the QA room CC did a quick recap of her lunch hour, perplexed by the range of feelings and emotions Liz had gone through in such a short period of time. She concluded that although the roller coaster effect was somewhat unsettling, she was more than ready for the ride. Dating Elizabeth McLeary was probably not going to be easy, but it certainly was not going to be boring.

* * *

She wouldn't have been able to explain why, but for some reason the afternoon found CC able to focus on work. By three p.m. she'd gone through every potential lead of her assigned campaigns. She knew Beth was overwhelmed working on qualifying surveys for a large market research campaign. The campaign had started the day before and was to be completed within one week so half the reps were working on it, generating an impressive number of surveys. Beth would never be able to go through them alone without working overtime. CC would have offered to help under any circumstances, but she was even more eager to assist Beth today, thinking a little ass-kissing couldn't hurt after what had happened that morning.

CC approached Beth's desk carefully. Although she'd never seen her boss as cold as she'd been a few hours earlier, she'd seen her under stress, and Beth was definitely under stress today. That meant she was grumpy as hell and CC didn't feel the need to get her head bitten off again. Staying a safe distance from Beth, she watched for a few seconds as a leg bounced frenetically up and down under her desk. She was about to explode.

"Idiots," she muttered to herself, still unaware of CC's presence. "All a bunch of idiots."

"Beth?" CC risked. When Beth showed no reaction, CC moved close enough to enter her peripheral vision, obstructed by a mass of long, dark blond hair. "Beth?"

This time Beth turned her attention to CC. "They have no idea what market research is, Ciel. I'm about to lose my mind. They're supposed to read the damn questions verbatim. No prompting, no leading. How hard is that, really? But I can't blame them. They were trained by the same moron who sends the client every survey I disqualify. I don't even know why I bother."

"Let me guess. Jeff Hudson?"

"Who else? How can a man be so stupid, Ciel? I don't understand how so much stupidity can fit in one tiny little brain."

Beth was clearly upset, but CC couldn't help but grin. "One of the most mind-boggling mysteries of this world, no doubt. Some day his name will be in medical textbooks. Mark my word."

Beth laughed. A quiet, breathy laugh that brought color to her normally pale cheeks and exposed pristine white teeth. Her laughter was brief but followed by a heavy sigh of relief. "Thank you, Ciel. I needed that." Her eyes were tender again, the eyes CC was used to and had been missing more than she thought possible during the last few hours.

"Anytime. I was just coming to see if you needed help, actually."

Another sigh escaped Beth, followed by the slow blinking CC was hoping for. "If I were a hugger I'd hug you right now. I'll never get through this crap on my own."

"All right then. Where do I start?"

"I started at the top of the alphabet so you start at the bottom and we meet in the middle?"

"Sounds good." Beth and CC had often shared QA on a campaign in similar circumstances. It was the closest they came to teamwork in the department. CC enjoyed it very much. She was looking forward to reaching the record that would already bear Beth's initials, indicating their task was done. "Do we listen to all of the recordings?"

"No. We listen to fifty percent and correct grammar and spelling on all of them. Believe me; listening to half of them is more than frustrating enough."

"I bet. Okay, let's get to it then." CC turned to go back to her own cubicle but Beth gently grabbed her hand to stop her. Beth seemed as surprised by the touch as CC and quickly brought her hand back to her desk where she fiddled nervously with a pen. In the two years she'd been working with Beth, CC couldn't recall another instance of physical contact. Beth was the kind of person who needed a very wide circle of personal space around her, and CC had always respected that. "Was there something else?"

Beth looked at the pen she was twisting between her long fingers and took a deep breath before she turned back to CC. "Yes. I just wanted to say I'm sorry about this morning. I've been very stressed out with this campaign and I may have overreacted."

CC didn't expect an apology, but she was touched by Beth's honesty. "It's okay. No need to apologize. I know the rules and it won't happen again."

Beth's smile was tentative. "Okay. So, we're good?"

"We're good. You're still the best boss there is."

Beth looked down to the pen still twirling in her hand. A perplexing look on her face.

"What else is on your mind? Whatever it is, you can say it, Beth."

Beth hesitated and closed her eyes for a long moment. When she opened them again, they looked straight into CC's. "It's really none of my business, Ciel, but please be careful with that girl."

Beth's plea shocked CC even more than her touch. They'd never talked about their personal lives. CC didn't know if Beth was dating anyone or even what kind of man she found attractive. She assumed she was not married because she didn't wear a ring, but she knew nothing of Beth's love life. Just as Beth knew nothing of hers. CC had never talked about Michelle when they were dating or about any other woman she might have been interested in since then. Actually CC had never even come out to Beth. If she knew she was gay, it had to be because she had overheard something or had come to her own conclusions based on her own observations. The fact that Beth was warning her about Liz now puzzled her, but she couldn't help but feel that if Beth had chosen to cross this barrier between them, it had to be important.

"Why? Is there something you know that I should know?"

Beth bit her bottom lip as if trying to take back her warning. Much, much too late. "No. Nothing specific. Just a feeling. She rubs me the wrong way, I guess." She hesitated but continued in one breath, "I care about you, Ciel, and I don't want to see you get hurt."

CC felt confused, a little worried and a little annoyed. She didn't know if Beth was some kind of witch who could sense in Liz something awful CC couldn't see yet or some kind of bitch who felt entitled to stick her nose in her business. Her tone was flat when she spoke, "Okay, well, thank you, I guess. I appreciate your concern and I'll take your warning into consideration."

With that she turned away and walked back to her own cubicle, deflated. She heard Beth sigh with frustration and when she sat down in front of her computer an email had already arrived from her.

CC opened the message and read the two lines with a heavy heart. "I'm sorry, please forget I said anything. It's really none of my business. –B"

CC deleted the email without replying and attacked the market research database, starting in the Zs.

* * *

When the intercom buzzed in her loft shortly after six, CC was finally able to let go of Beth's warning and revel in the excitement of her upcoming date. "Come on up," she said before running to the bathroom for one more look in the mirror. She wore a deep blue square-neck T-shirt with her best pair of jeans. Her thick and silky hair smelled like wild cherry blossom shampoo and a touch of mascara highlighted her eyes. Her look was casual, but it was clear she'd put more effort into it than she would for the workday. She nodded at herself with a semi-satisfied grin. Not too bad. The knock at the door concluded her appraisal and she hurried to welcome Liz.

"Hi," Liz said with a smile as she entered the loft, carrying in one hand a plastic bag from which delicious aromas of Thai food escaped and in the other a large object that CC guessed was the painting Liz wanted to her to see. It measured approximately two feet by three feet and was carefully wrapped in brown paper, not yet ready to be unveiled.

"Hi. Come in, let me get this." CC took the bag from Liz's hand and brought it to the kitchen.

"I got shrimp pad thai. I hope you're not allergic to seafood or peanuts."

"No allergies for me. This smells delicious." Liz put her parcel down and set it against the wall before following CC to the kitchen area of the loft. When CC turned around Liz was just inches away and the sight of her took her breath away.

"You look amazing." Liz's red hair was falling down her back, a dark brown halter top showcased beautifully freckled shoulders and skinny white jeans hugged her curves perfectly. Her eye makeup was impeccable, and the gloss on her full lips was ridiculously inviting.

"Thanks, so do you." Liz's gaze travelled down to CC's mouth and CC swallowed hard, grateful when Liz's focus shifted to her surroundings. "And so does your place. Wow, it looks like we have the same taste in the home design department."

"Thank you. I really love it here. Wine?"

"Please." CC took two wine glasses out of the cupboard and grabbed the bottle of Riesling that was chilling in the refrigerator. Liz seemed nervous, almost restless, which, strangely, had a calming effect on CC. She offered Liz a slow, lazy smile that was rewarded with a shy grin and the question, "Anything I can do to help?"

"You could get that painting unwrapped while I pour the wine. I'm dying to see it." Liz's smile lost its timidity at the request and her entire expression became one of joy. CC mused that she'd never seen eyes really sparkle before, but when Liz was really happy or excited about something a million tiny diamonds pierced through the emerald green of her eyes.

"Okay, I don't usually show my work, but this one I can't wait to show you." She walked to the painting and CC poured the wine, listening to the sound of paper being torn enthusiastically. Soon Liz came back to the kitchen with a large ball of brown paper. "Recycling?"

"Yeah, right here." She opened a small pantry where a recycling bin was sitting on the floor. When Liz freed her hands of the paper, CC handed her a glass of wine that she accepted with a thank-you.

"So, ready to see it?"

Liz's eagerness reminded CC of her own innocent fervor every time she would come home with one of the many drawings her parents displayed on their refrigerator all through her childhood. "Absolutely." Wine glass in one hand, Liz used her free hand to take CC's and led her to the painting that was still leaning against the white wall next to the door.

CC almost dropped her own glass of wine when she stopped in front of the canvas, which was covered with what must have been all existing shades of blue known to mankind. With faint touches of white, black, and gray, the multiple hues of blue dominated the painting. They took different shapes if you looked at them closely, but they all came together to form large concentric circles if you took the artwork as a whole. CC saw the ocean, the sky, maybe a cyclone, light, darkness and depth. So much depth. She was mesmerized. She realized Liz was studying her reaction closely and took a deep breath so she could speak, still staring at the painting. "It's amazing, Liz. So beautiful."

Liz sighed loudly and CC wondered how long she'd been holding her breath. "Really? You like it?"

"I love it. I see so many things in there. I can't even explain it. It really gets to me." She brought her hand to her chest and closed it into a fist in an attempt to physically express what the artwork made her feel.

"You're not just saying that to be nice, are you?"

"No, I promise. I really, really love it." CC managed to take her eyes off the painting to turn to Liz and raise her glass. "I propose a toast to a very talented artist."

"Thank you. It means the world to me that you really like it." They clinked their glasses together and took a small sip of wine before Liz continued. "Especially since you were my inspiration."

CC brought her attention back to the artwork, looking for something different in it. Something she'd missed. "Me? How?"

"I started working on it the day I met you. It's everything, every color and every temperature I've seen in your eyes in the five short days I've known you."

CC remained in front of the painting, speechless. She stared, trying desperately to recognize herself in any way, wondering how she could possibly inspire such art. She felt Liz's hand travel from her neck down her back before it finally rested on her hip. Her body warmed up when Liz tenderly pressed her lips against her cheek. She was overwhelmed, and it was only when she tasted the saltiness of her own tears on her lip that she was able to swallow the lump in her throat and speak in a voice that was barely audible, "But it's so beautiful."

Liz quickly moved to the space between CC and the painting, forcing CC to redirect her gaze from the blue canvas to her. Both of her arms were now around CC's waist, her glass of wine nicely cooling CC's lower back, and their foreheads were touching. "So are you, sweetheart. Don't you get it? This painting doesn't even do you justice."

CC watched Liz's mouth as she spoke the words and wasn't surprised when that mouth brushed against hers. She loved the taste of Liz's lips mixed with her tears. The kiss was soft and gentle, and CC let Liz take her hand and lead her back to the kitchen area where their food was getting cold despite the heat that radiated from CC's entire being.

CHAPTER SEVEN

"I didn't know you smoke," CC told Liz as she watched the redhead use the sole of her high-heeled shoe to put out a cigarette she'd just smoked nearly down to its filter before throwing it to the ground.

"It's an on and off thing I do." Liz sat down next to CC on the bench they'd chosen for lunch in a park near the office the Monday after their first date. CC categorized the date as successful. She'd been moved by Liz's painting and even more thrilled when Liz had given her the canvas when the evening ended. It was by far the most thoughtful present she'd ever received from any woman she'd dated, especially on the very first date. They'd shared a few more kisses after dinner but had remained surprisingly chaste despite the growing heat between them. Today they'd walked together to the park after stopping at Marcel's, the popular sandwich shop across the street from D&B, to get food for their impromptu picnic. CC was on cloud nine. They watched a couple run past them on the running and biking trail they were facing as they settled on their bench with matching chicken salad on wheat sandwiches and Diet Cokes. "I know. I need to quit again. It's a gross habit."

Afraid Liz had interpreted her comment as an accusation, CC decided to come clean regarding her own habit. "I was not judging. I'm in no position to judge since I smoke pot on a regular basis."

"You do?" Liz asked with eyebrows raised in incredulity and a certain twinkle in her eye.

"I have for years. You didn't know? I thought Kayla made it her life mission to tell everyone at work," CC declared sarcastically.

"Kayla and I don't talk much," Liz said with a hint of sadness in her eyes before taking a bite of her sandwich. CC made a note to herself to ask Kayla what that was about. Kayla talked to everyone. Liz focused on another runner who had just passed in front of them on the trail. This one was a woman running with a large dog. All they could see was her back, but she looked healthy and oh so cool in her black running shorts and purple sleeveless top. CC couldn't help but notice her perfect runner's ass, round and so firm it barely moved—so unlike her own—and glanced at Liz just in time to see that she'd noticed too. "Do you think we could do this?" Liz asked.

CC turned back to the runner who was about to disappear behind the trees lining the trail as it curved deeper into the park. "What? Running?"

"Yeah."

"With a lot of training, maybe."

CC watched as Liz turned sideways on the bench to face her with a suddenly animated expression: her eyes were wide open, her smile was blinding and she grabbed CC's shoulders tightly as she spoke. "We should do it. I quit smoking, you quit pot and we start running. What do you say? Deal?"

Liz's enthusiasm was overwhelming but also contagious, and before she realized what she was doing CC found herself agreeing. "Okay, let's do it. I'll find us a training schedule on the Internet," she heard the nerd in her say.

She was rewarded with a hug that made it hard for her to breathe before full lips took hold of hers in a kiss that lacked focus but made up for it with strength and energy. "We're gonna be total babes, CC. God, I'm so excited! We start tomorrow?"

"Yeah, tomorrow sounds good." CC giggled at Liz's pure excitement. They finished their lunch making plans for their new lifestyle, deciding to go to the mall after work to get decent running shoes as well as some athletic clothing. Liz went on about everything they could do if they were healthier, like hiking the Adirondacks and biking across New York State. CC felt dizzy and somewhat disarmed. The question that often popped into her mind after she spent time with Liz came back again. *What the hell just happened?* As they walked back to work she smiled at the thought of becoming the healthier version of herself she'd always wanted to be. Then her thoughts became slightly nostalgic and she vowed to savor every puff of her last joint, which she planned on smoking that night.

* * *

"No, thank you," CC said for the third time as Kayla tried again to hand her the blunt she was smoking on their drive to work. It was Friday morning and the beginning of CC's fourth day without marijuana. She'd skipped her usual visit at Kayla's and Damon's the previous night. Instead she'd gone to the park with Liz for their second run of the week. In all honesty, there was not much running involved yet. CC had found a schedule for beginners that started with intervals between walking and running and would gradually, after several weeks of training, allow them to run five kilometers continuously. CC was still skeptical since she felt like she could die after a single full minute of running. For the first week of training their schedule outlined three training sessions, each session requiring them to complete seven intervals of walking for three minutes and running for one minute. A total of seven minutes running didn't seem that difficult, but their first two sessions had left CC exhausted, sweatier than she'd ever been and unexpectedly proud. She'd never imagined she could some day become a runner, but now she could see it happen and she liked the idea. She also liked that she was doing it with a partner who encouraged her every step of the way. Liz's ambition appeared to be endless and fed CC's own motivation on a daily basis.

"Sorry CC. I can't get used to your new health freak ways. Are you serious about this shit?"

"Very serious."

"You're not doing it for her, are you? 'Cuz if she doesn't like you the way you are, she can go fuck herself, right?"

The comment reminded CC of Liz's sadness when she'd mentioned Kayla in the park, and she decided now was as good a time as any to question her friend. "I think we're both doing it for ourselves and each other actually. But why are you concerned about it? Do you have a problem with Liz?"

Kayla breathed the marijuana smoke and held it in for an eternity before finally breathing out the window. *Sure, now you want to think before you talk*, CC mused as she waited for Kayla's answer. "Truth is, I don't know if I really have a problem with her yet, but I sure can't say I like her either."

"Why not?" CC asked weakly. She knew the answer that Kayla gave her would be as straightforward as they come.

"I can't put my finger on it, or I would've told you about it already. I just don't trust her. There's something off about her, just sayin'."

CC was surprised by Kayla's uncertainty, but her words were enough to bring Beth's warning to mind, something she'd not thought about in a week. A knot lodged itself in her throat. First Beth, now Kayla. Was she missing something about the woman she was quickly falling in love with? Was she blinded by her attraction to her, her feelings for her?

No, it had to be the other way around. She remembered the painting, Liz's touch, their kisses, their conversations, their plans, the light in those intense green eyes, and she knew she was right. Beth and Kayla were the ones who didn't see the real Liz, her Liz. Her tone was calm but determined when she addressed

Kayla. "Well, if you ever know anything concrete, please let me know. But in the meantime I would really appreciate if you made the effort to at least try to like her. Because I do, K. I really, really like her."

Kayla put her blunt away as they approached the office, and she sighed deeply, considering CC's request. "How much do you like her, for real?"

The question was asked with a grin that was softer, less sarcastic than usual, and CC understood she could be honest with her friend. She couldn't help the smile that appeared on her face as she looked for the right words to express her feelings for Liz. "She's good for me, Kayla. She makes me reach for more. She stimulates me in every possible way: physically, intellectually and emotionally. I'm falling in love with her. Plain and simple." Her voice broke as she finished her sentence, and she felt her cheeks warm up with a blush.

"Holy fuck, baby girl, you've got it bad," Kayla said before she snickered in her usual way. Then she sighed again and took on a serious, sincere expression, something CC had rarely seen on her face. "All right, CC. I'll try. For you. But you have to know I'm keeping my bullshit radar on. And that's cuz you're my friend, I love you and it's my job to look out for you. All right?" Kayla patted CC's thigh in a rare sign of affection.

"Okay. That works."

"All right then. I still hate that you ain't smoking no more, by the way. Carrot-Bitch may be good for you, but she makes you boring." They laughed, and CC couldn't help but feel grateful for Kayla's friendship, realizing it might be deeper than she'd thought. She was glad she had a woman like Kayla in her corner.

* * *

CC was still going through her work emails when Beth arrived fifteen minutes after she and Kayla had started working. Strangely enough, she found that it took her longer to find her focus without a morning buzz. When she was more alert, she needed a moment to get her thoughts organized for the day.

"Breakfast is here, ladies. Happy Friday," Beth declared in her normal cheerful morning mood. "Ciel, I know you didn't want a bagel, so I got you something else." Beth continued to her cubicle where she knew Kayla and CC would go get their breakfast. CC's new lifestyle included healthier eating habits, and she'd told Beth about her efforts to politely explain her request not to bring her a bagel on Fridays anymore. She'd also mentioned that she would no longer drink hazelnut coffee with cream and that if Beth insisted on bringing her coffee, which was not necessary, of course, she would go for regular coffee with skim milk from now on.

CC walked to Beth's cubicle, where Kayla was already going through the bag of goodies, taking out different flavors of yogurt and a variety of fresh fruit with such disgust that CC couldn't help but chuckle. "It's not funny, CC. You've ruined our boss and Friday's breakfast, you health freak. I hate you."

Although she said it with humor, CC knew there was some truth to Kayla's comment. Apparently Beth had decided she'd suffered enough. "Don't worry, Kayla. I didn't forget about you." She produced another, smaller paper bag she'd been hiding behind her back and handed it to Kayla. "Here's your bagel and cream cheese."

"Oh thank god, I thought I was gonna have to starve with you granola bitches. Thank you, boss."

"You're most welcome," Beth answered with a laugh as Kayla disappeared out of the room with her breakfast. CC approached the food Beth had brought with awe at the woman's thoughtfulness. "I didn't know which one you'd prefer so I brought a few options. My favorite is this Greek yogurt, here." She held a small yogurt tub in her hand. "It has more protein than the others, which is really important, but I'm sure you know that."

"Not really. I mean I started doing research and I'm learning, but it looks like you may have a lot to teach me," CC said with a warm smile. She thought Beth might be blushing but could not say with certainty.

"Well, if you have any questions, ask me. I'll be happy to tell you what I know. For breakfast I usually have this yogurt with some fresh fruit. Oh and I put some of these in my yogurt too, for more fiber and Omega-3. But that's up to you." She held a small bag of seeds CC did not recognize. She had to take the bag from Beth's hands to read the label that identified the mysterious content as flaxseed.

"Thank you so much. I know I sound like a broken record, but you didn't have to do this. When I asked you not to bring me a bagel it was just so you wouldn't waste a bagel. I really didn't expect you to bring all this."

"You should know me better than that by now, Ciel," Beth said with a smirk and a pink color on her cheeks that CC could finally identify as a definite blush.

"You're right. I should." CC wanted to add that they really should know each other a lot better after working so closely for two years, but she didn't. Instead she silently wondered for the millionth time why and whose fault it was that they in fact knew so little about each other. "And what about you? Where's your breakfast?"

"Oh, I'll have yogurt and fruit, like you. I eat this way most of the time anyway so I can live without my Friday bagel."

"Oh no, please don't change your habits for me, Beth. It's not like you can't afford a bagel. I mean, look at you." CC quickly let her gaze travel down Beth's body to make her point and couldn't help but turn warm as she realized how beautiful a body it truly was: lean and athletic yet curvaceous in all the right places. When her attention came back to her boss's face she saw that Beth's own blush had intensified. "I'm sorry, I hope I didn't make you uncomfortable. I just meant that a bagel won't hurt you."

"I know, Ciel. And I'll have my bagel this weekend, don't worry. But right now I'll eat yogurt with you. I know changing your eating habits is very hard, I've been there, so I'll do all I can to support you."

"Thank you." CC watched as Beth blinked slowly and smiled at her, amazed yet again at the woman's kindness. "So, how much of that flaxseed stuff do I need?"

"I'll show you." Beth fixed CC's breakfast as she explained the benefits of each fruit she'd brought. CC went back to her cubicle with a healthy breakfast and a regular coffee with skim milk, pledging internally to make more of an effort to really get to know Beth.

* * *

Although CC had spent many Friday nights alone in her loft before, this one hurt. Liz had left for Saratoga right after work to spend the weekend with her family and CC already missed her very much. It was also the first time since quitting that she really missed marijuana. A joint had always been her way to celebrate the arrival of the weekend and she didn't quite know what to do instead. She grabbed the lesbian romance novel she hadn't read yet and tried to settle down in the window seat, but she felt restless. She went to the kitchen for a glass of water and decided a walk might help. She put on her running shoes, grabbed her keys and iPod, and exited her loft with a spring in her step. She took the stairs to the ground floor and stopped in the lobby to get her earphones perfectly right, a task that always tested her obsessive-compulsive tendencies. She was selecting a playlist when she heard her mother's voice calling her through the door. "Hey, honey, were you on your way out?" The surprise was obvious in her voice, matched with equal joy. CC looked up to see her parents on the sidewalk and let them into the lobby.

"Yeah, I was going for a walk. Would you like to join me?"

"Sure, that's a great idea," Marie said before she hugged her daughter and kissed her on the cheek.

Charles hugged CC as well before he answered with less enthusiasm than his wife, "Okay, why not? Just let me put this wine back in the car." He held the door of the building open for Marie and CC and put the wine in the car that was parked on the street, and they all started walking at a respectable pace, following the Mohawk River toward the Cohoes Falls. "I don't remember you going for a walk before, baby. Is this a new thing?" Charles asked his daughter. His long stride was slow and awkward. CC's father was no athlete and even walking looked strange on him.

"Yes, very new. I just started this week. And I even do some running, believe it or not."

"Good for you, Ciel," her mother chimed in. "As long as it's not to lose weight. There's nothing wrong with your body, honey."

"It's not just to lose weight, mom. Don't get me wrong, if I do lose some I'll be very happy. But it's more than that. I want to be healthier. I want to better myself. Exercise is only one part of it. Actually, you might disown me for this, but I also quit smoking weed."

"You're kidding me," Charles said, frozen into place on the sidewalk.

CC walked back to her father and took hold of his arm. "I'm not kidding, Dad. I really want to become healthier and my lungs are part of the equation. My brains too."

"I get it." Marie grabbed Charles's free arm and they started walking again. "I get it and I'm very proud of you for making these changes. We'll support you in any way we can, honey, as long as you don't expect us to stop too. I'm afraid your old parents will die as a couple of pothead hippies."

"You bet we will," Charles added with a grin. They laughed in unison.

"I'm not asking anyone to change, guys, don't worry. So how have you been? Are you enjoying your summer off, Dad? Have you convinced Mom to retire yet?" CC asked with a wink.

Charles sighed heavily, obviously frustrated. "No luck there, baby. Your mom is as stubborn as they come."

"Oh please, not that again. One of my patients tried to kill herself this week. She needs me, Charles. They all need me." CC regretted asking the question that so instantly created tension, but she wasn't sure how to lighten up the mood. Fortunately they were arriving at the falls and her mother easily redirected everyone's attention to happier thoughts. It was a gift she had.

"Oh God, look how beautiful it is. I can't believe we have these amazing falls right here in our town and we never come to enjoy them properly. Thanks for suggesting this walk, honey. It was a wonderful idea." Marie put her arms around CC's shoulders and squeezed her daughter tightly against her. They stood quietly for a few minutes, taking in the natural beauty of the falls, which were ninety feet tall and a thousand feet wide. The water flow was low at this time of the year compared to springtime when the falls were most impressive, but the view was still well worth the short walk. CC promised herself she would come back soon.

"I'm glad you came with me. Next time maybe we can go to Peebles Island. I haven't been there in ages."

"Great, count me in," said Marie. They started walking back toward the old cotton mill at a slower pace, as if the falls had left them calmer, more relaxed. "So what else is new with my beautiful daughter? I feel like there's something else you're not telling us."

CC hesitated because her relationship with Liz was still so new, but in the end she couldn't keep the news from her parents, especially knowing how happy it would make them. "Well, I've been kind of seeing someone." She spoke the words as casually as she could, but her parents still stopped walking and stared at her in shock.

"What? And you're just now telling us?" Marie asked as Charles pulled his daughter into a warm embrace.

"I knew there had to be more behind this weird walking and running and quitting pot of yours. So, tell us about this girl, baby."

"Her name is Liz. We met at work. And it's still very new, so there's not much to tell yet." CC started walking again as she spoke, forcing her parents to follow her so they would not miss a word.

"There has to be more though. Come on, Ciel, give us something." Her mother's plea made CC smile.

"What do you want to know?"

"Everything!" Marie exclaimed impatiently. "What does she do? How old is she? What does she look like? What does she want in life?"

"Whoa, Mom, stop. You're giving me a headache. One thing at a time okay? She's a phone rep right now but only for the summer. She's studying business, and she's also a very talented artist. She's twenty-four. She's beautiful, Mom, she takes my breath away. And I don't know everything she wants in life yet. Right now we're working on getting healthier together. It's nice. Really, really nice."

Marie grabbed CC's hand and laced their fingers together. "I'm so happy for you, honey. So when do we get to meet her?"

CC laughed out loud at her mother's eagerness. "I don't know, Mom. It's way too early to meet the parents."

Marie put out her bottom lip, pouting dramatically before she squeezed CC's hand and conceded, "I understand, I guess. But don't wait too long, okay?"

"I promise."

They arrived in front of her building and Charles grabbed the wine out of the car. "Why don't we celebrate this great news with a glass of wine? Or is this against your new religion too?" he asked, winking teasingly at CC.

"One glass won't hurt me. Come on up."

Marie hesitated before following CC toward the stairwell, but Charles remained planted in front of the elevator and hit the up button. "You go right ahead, ladies, but I'll stick with the elevator. They were invented for a very good reason, after all. This great bottle of Chardonnay and I will meet you upstairs."

CHAPTER EIGHT

"Are you going to that thing next month?" Kayla asked CC on their way to work the following Friday. Sign-up sheets for the Dixon & Brown's annual dinner-cruise on Lake George had been pinned to the board of the breakroom earlier that week, but CC had not added her name to the list yet. It was one of two annual parties the company organized to thank its employees, the second one being the mandatory holiday party.

"I guess. I usually go, even though being trapped on a boat for hours with most of the people we work with terrifies me," CC answered with a grin to soften her declaration.

"Good, make sure you save some time for me."

CC detected a hint of accusation in Kayla's tone. "Of course, K. Why wouldn't I have time for you? You're one of the three people I actually talk to. You're the social butterfly here." She pointed her thumb at Kayla without taking her hand off the steering wheel before adding, "Not *moi*."

Kayla sucked on her blunt aggressively and didn't seem to take any pleasure in it. She quickly blew out the smoke and transferred her hostility to her voice when she spoke. "Well, one of the three people you talk to seems to take all of your time lately. Just sayin'. I mean, for real, just cuz you quit smoking weed don't mean you can't hang out with us any more right? Damon was hoping to see you last night. It was the second week you skipped. That makes him feel like he was nothing more than your dealer, CC, and he thought he was your friend."

CC was taken aback by Kayla's rant. She'd heard her talk to and about other people that way, but her abrasiveness had never been directed at her before. It left her speechless for a moment. Then she realized what Kayla was saying. She missed the little time they spent together outside of work. Damon missed her visits. They were friends, real friends that she'd put aside for a new relationship. How cliché.

"You're right. I'm sorry, K. We've been dating for three weeks so it's still very new and exciting, but that's no excuse. I miss Damon too. Let's have dinner some time soon, okay?" She dared a glance at Kayla and was pleased when she saw one corner of her mouth go up in a half grin.

"Okay, what about tomorrow? We have nothing planned."

CC winced. "Oh, I can't tomorrow. Liz and I already have plans. She's supposed to spend the night at my place..." CC swallowed nervously before she continued, "for the first time."

Kayla snickered and CC was happy to hear the low, evil sound, despite the fact it was at her expense. "Are you telling me you and Carrot-Bitch haven't done it yet, CC? What the fuck are you waiting for?"

"We just started dating, K. We're taking it slow. What's the rush?" CC felt defensive.

"The rush is we need to know if the carpet matches the drapes, baby girl. Don't you wanna know if your woman is a real fire crotch?"

"Shut up!" CC playfully slapped Kayla's thigh before they both burst out laughing. They kept laughing until they reached their destination. CC parked her Jetta and turned to Kayla before exiting the car. "Thank you for understanding. And thank you for calling me out on my crap. Let's do dinner next week okay?"

Kayla's smile was warm when she faced CC. "Okay. Let me check with Damon and I'll let you know what works." She grabbed CC's hand and squeezed it firmly before letting it go so quickly CC was not sure what happened. "I'm happy for you, CC. For real."

"Thank you. And I promise I'll make more time for you and Damon. You're the only friends I have and you're very important to me. Don't ever doubt that again okay?"

"All right now, don't get all sappy on me, woman. Let's get to work. And if Beth brings me a yogurt you're dead to me, is that clear?"

"Clear as day." Kayla lit up a Marlboro Light as she exited the car and they walked slowly to the building, giving her enough time to smoke half her cigarette.

* * *

Saturday night started well enough. CC and Liz shared a delicious meal and a nice bottle of Chianti in a quaint Italian restaurant not too far from CC's and walked back to the old cotton mill at a leisurely pace. Liz talked about her passion for art, the business classes she planned on taking in the fall, her obsession with eighties music and Tori Amos's entire body of work. The whole time she talked the million diamonds in her eyes danced with anticipation. CC focused not only on those eyes but on every feature of her girlfriend's beautiful face. The slight cleft in her chin she'd already kissed too many times to count, the soft tongue that peeked out and licked full pink lips when she stopped talking for a rare second, the cheeks that flushed subtly at every brush of their hands, accidental or not.

When they entered the loft they kissed. At first they kissed the same way they'd kissed since their first date: soft and sensual. But tonight CC wanted more. They'd decided Liz would spend the night and although it hadn't been said explicitly, to CC that meant they were going to make love. She was so ready for it. They'd been working out for three weeks and she'd lost five pounds. She already felt better in her own skin and that newfound confidence, mixed with a desire that had been very well fed for the past few weeks, made her uncharacteristically assertive. She pushed her tongue into Liz's mouth and slowly but thoroughly explored it, groaning with satisfaction when a moan escaped Liz and vibrated against her lips. Liz's hands penetrated her thick hair and held her possessively against her mouth, demanding more. CC felt wetness and throbbing between her legs and pushed her pelvis against Liz, pinning her to the wall. She continued kissing Liz forcefully, hearing heavy breathing and panting that she interpreted as sounds of pleasure—until Liz shoved her abruptly with both hands and ran to the bathroom. Liz closed and locked the door behind her before CC even had time to realize what had happened.

Her passion died instantly, and she felt cold so deep inside she could swear her blood froze in her veins. She felt tears run down her cheeks and was shocked at their warmth. Tiny, sharp cubes of ice would have been more appropriate. Liz had rejected her and she'd been completely blindsided. She, the same CC who'd spent all of her life fearing and expecting rejection, had been dismissed in perhaps the only moment she hadn't foreseen it. In the only moment she'd felt confident and sure of herself. What a fucking slap in the face, really.

She fought her need to crawl into bed and dragged her feet to the bathroom instead, dreading yet needing an explanation. She placed an ear against the door and listened. She heard water running but could also detect sobbing. Her heart broke again, this time at the thought she was the reason behind the tears of the woman she loved and because she had no clue what she'd done wrong. She finally knocked on the door, so lightly she almost sounded like a dog scratching, begging to be let inside.

"Liz, what's going on?" Her voice cracked. She hadn't noticed her own tears had kept flowing. She sniffled before she continued in a pleading voice, "What did I do?"

"No-thing, it's-not-you." Each syllable was accentuated with a heart-wrenching sob. Each breath and each sound seemed to be excruciatingly painful. "I-just-need...time." Even more violent bawling followed.

Feeling powerless on the other side of the door, CC did the only thing she could do. "Okay, okay. Don't talk. Take all the time you need. I'll be right here waiting for you." She kept her ear against the door until Liz's hysterical crying simmered down to a point where she was at least breathing more regularly. Then she let her body slip down to the floor and leaned her back against the bathroom door. And she waited.

* * *

CC guessed she'd been waiting for about half an hour when she heard Liz unlock the door. She quickly jumped to her feet and turned around to face the door when it opened. Liz appeared with a timid smile, embarrassed. Her eyes were swollen and red. Tear streaks marked her face. The hair that had been pulled back in a sleek and elegant ponytail now had unruly red strands sticking out in several places.

"I'm sorry," she let out in a breath as she walked into CC's arms.

CC welcomed her in a comforting embrace and simply held her in silence, relieved that she was allowed to do so, content to feel the woman's body against hers. She hesitated before she spoke, but she couldn't act like nothing had happened. "No need to apologize. But tell me what happened. Please."

Liz tightened her hold around CC's waist and CC granted the wordless request to simply be held a little while longer. They stood in the hall just like that, hugging and rocking each other until Liz stepped away, took CC's hand and led her to the couch where they sat together. Liz sat with her back leaning against CC's body. She was trembling. CC instinctively put her arm around her and Liz used it like a blanket, wrapping herself with it and holding on as tightly as she could.

"I will tell you, sweetheart. But it's very hard for me, and it's been so long since I told anyone I'm not sure how it's going to come out."

CC would have preferred seeing Liz's eyes and the expression on her face as she spoke, but she understood by the way Liz chose to sit that she couldn't look at her. She respected her choice.

"It's okay. Take your time. I just want to understand." She held on to the armrest of the couch with her free hand, bracing herself for what Liz had to say.

"When you kissed me earlier, I was really into it." CC didn't respond. She had a feeling it would take a while before anything Liz said made sense and interrupting or redirecting her would only make things worse. "God, CC, I wanted to fuck you so bad I could taste it."

CC ignored the twinge in her sex and tightened her hold on the armrest. *You didn't run to the bathroom because you wanted to fuck me*, she wanted to say. She remained quiet.

"But then when you pushed me against the wall I felt trapped. Exactly like I did when he held me against the cot in the basement and then it's like I wasn't with you anymore. I was there, in that fucking basement."

CC grimaced as Liz squeezed her arm so tightly that her nails were digging into flesh, but she ignored the pain. Instead of taking her arm away she let go of the armrest so she could hold Liz closer, with both arms. Liz nestled against her.

CC had heard too many horror stories of children being molested from her mother, whose patients had too often barely survived such abuse, not to imagine the worst as she heard Liz's words. But she still had many questions. It was getting very difficult to remain silent.

Liz's tone was surprisingly calm, detached. "I was five. That summer my parents thought it'd be nice for me to spend time with my grandparents so they sent me there instead of day care while they worked. I remember I cried because I wanted to go to day care with my friend Alice."

Liz turned to look at CC and smiled at her. CC was alarmed by what she saw. The smile was lifeless, completely fake. The green eyes were glazed and without any real focus, as if there was nothing behind them. She was relieved when Liz turned back around and leaned against her again, hiding her expression or lack thereof. Liz was not with her. Her body was there, telling a story, but Liz was hidden deep inside. *Protecting herself,* she thought. CC wished her arms could reach inside and hold her soul, but instead she kept holding on to Liz's empty shell as she continued her narration.

"After a couple of weeks I forgot all about Alice. My grandparents were really nice, especially my grandfather. He took me everywhere with him, called me his 'precious little baby girl.' My parents were kind of cold so I really liked the attention. He bought me pretty dresses, cute shoes, all kinds of things. He spoiled me and I loved every minute of it."

She paused. CC waited patiently for the rest of the story, hoping against all hopes it was not going the way she knew it was.

"My grandparents' neighbors had a boy about my age. Dan. He was nice and we played together once in a while. When my grandfather was too busy to play with me. One day Dan and I were in the basement and we started playing a different kind of game. 'Show me yours and I'll show you mine,' you know what I mean." Liz's phony laugh chilled CC's blood. "It was so innocent. Just a couple of kids playing doctor. But when my grandfather found us with our pants down to our knees he went nuts. He sent Dan home and started yelling at me. 'You little slut,' he kept saying. He looked so different, so angry. I think I said I was sorry, but I'm not sure. I was so scared. He got closer to me and started breathing heavily in my face, staring at the parts of me that were nude. I remember his eyes were black and his breath smelled of peppermint and garlic mixed together. I'd never heard someone breathe so loud. Then he lifted me off the floor and took me to that old rusty iron cot that was sitting in a corner of the basement. He put my arms over my head and held me there, with one huge hand around my wrists. It hurt so bad, CC. That's what I remember the most. How bad my wrists hurt. Even though I knew his other hand was between my legs." She stopped talking and her body started shaking.

CC had heard enough, could not take anymore. She waited, almost hoping Liz would stop, her own body tensing when Liz's voice continued. "After that I never went back to my grandparents. I saw my grandmother once in a while, but not my grandfather. I think he didn't want to see me anymore. He died the following summer. Out of shame, I hope. Old bastard."

Liz suddenly got up and grabbed CC's hand to force her off the couch as well. CC looked into her eyes and saw that Liz was back with her, but the light in her eyes was pure fire, terrifying.

"That old bastard took enough from me, CC. I'm not going to let him take this too," she shouted as she waved her hand between herself and CC. "I love you and I want you and I'm going to fuck you just the way I want to. To hell with him," she declared between clenched teeth. She pulled on CC's arm and led her to the bedroom, where she fiercely pushed CC onto the bed. Liz's story had annihilated CC's libido; she didn't know how to handle the sudden rage in Liz or her own mixed feelings of disgust, resentment and sadness for what had happened to the woman that was now straddling her.

Before CC could gather her thoughts Liz had unzipped her jeans and plunged two fingers into her, taking her dry, fast and hard. The pain finally provoked a reaction from CC. "Stop!" she screamed. "Liz, stop!"

Liz ceased moving and her eyes locked onto CC's. The face that had been deformed by fury a second earlier transitioned to guilt and grief.

"Oh god, CC. I'm so sorry," she murmured as she withdrew her fingers carefully.

Speechless, CC kept studying Liz's face and watched as its features contorted again, this time with the ugliness of unguarded tears, of endless anguish. When Liz's body collapsed onto hers, she wrapped her arms around her and held her. Liz cried on CC's chest until she passed out, exhausted. CC listened to the reassuring sound of her deep, peaceful breathing for a long time before she let sleep claim her as well.

* * *

When CC woke up a few hours later, they were still in the same position. She felt warm under the weight of Liz's body, but

Liz was shivering. She started wiggling slowly, trying to think of the best way to move Liz under the covers without waking her up, but her attempt failed and Liz looked at her with a hesitant smile. "Sorry. I'm crushing you," she whispered as she let herself drop to the side.

"Not at all, but you're freezing. Let's move you under the covers." CC got up to pull down the bedclothes and took off her jeans before getting back into bed. Liz mimicked her and backed into CC, whose body immediately spooned her in return.

Liz took CC's hand and started playing with it, tracing its contours with her fingertips, slightly pulling each finger, caressing the palm. CC enjoyed the touch, which was not sexual but surely intimate.

"Do you think I'm crazy?"

The question surprised CC. "Crazy" was not a word she'd grown up with. She knew that too often in society it replaced words like "illness," "breakdown," "depression," "disorder" and so many more words that were familiar to her, but it was not a word she had or would ever use. It hadn't even come to mind despite the events of the night. Clearly Liz had been affected by what her grandfather had done to her, but that didn't make her crazy.

"No. I don't think you're crazy. I think something awful was done to you. Really, really awful." Liz said nothing else, and CC would have thought she was asleep if she hadn't kept playing with her hand. The tender touch was slowly putting CC to sleep until Liz turned around to face her.

CC felt Liz's arm snake around her waist. She opened her eyes and saw Liz's lips merely inches from her own when she whispered, "Make love to me, CC."

"What? Tonight? After everything?" CC was confused. She already felt dirty just from the chill that coursed through her body when she felt Liz's warm breath on her mouth. Surely they could not have sex after what Liz had shared with her. It was not appropriate. "I don't think it's a good idea. Let me just hold you tonight. Okay?"

Her resolve was threatened when Liz slid a hand under her T-shirt and started caressing her back and her side languorously. The redhead stared at her in the eyes and forced her to hold her gaze as she spoke calmly but determinately.

"No CC. What I tried to do earlier was not a good idea. It was all about him. It was wrong and I will never apologize enough for that. But what I want us to do now is right. I want to make love with you. I don't want us to be about him, about what he did to me. This isn't what tonight was supposed to be about. Please help me make it right. I need you to do this with me, CC. Please." Her whispered appeal dissolved CC's resistance. "Please," she said again as her hand traveled up CC's side until it covered the entire roundness of one breast. CC moaned as she felt her nipple push against Liz's palm in a yes she could not deny.

She took Liz's offered lips and their tongues and bodies pressed hard against each other and intertwined as if they couldn't get close enough. Every touch was slow and tender yet firm and purposeful, working toward a common goal to merge into something stronger, something that couldn't be destroyed by the past. They managed to undress each other without losing contact. One arm at a time. One leg at a time. There was no rush as long as they were holding on to each other. They kept their gazes fixed on one another. Blue on green, saying "I'm here. With you. This is about us." When they could finally feel the other's skin against the entire length of their bodies they stayed immobile for a long moment. Skin on skin. Their breathing grew erratic as they kept kissing, taking turns sucking on one another's tongue, as if trying to inhale the other.

Finally Liz rolled on top of CC and broke the seal between their mouths and upper bodies only enough to allow their sexes to meld. Wet folds blended and when their clitorises collided, they both gasped. Liz started riding CC, rubbing their sexes together more frantically. They groaned with pleasure, never losing eye contact, until their chests and faces were flushed with the red glow of orgasm and they came together.

Tears ran down Liz's cheeks as they had a few hours earlier, but this time they were running down to a satisfied smile, on a peaceful face. Again Liz's body collapsed onto her own, and CC covered both of them with the bedclothes before they fell asleep in a familiar position.

CHAPTER NINE

The end of July arrived with a heat wave that made the fifth week of their training schedule pure hell. On Monday Liz decided she wasn't running at temperatures over ninety degrees, and CC was very tempted to do the same. A nagging voice in her head, however, kept telling her that taking a break now would ruin all of her efforts, and although she muttered to the voice to shut the hell up, she still dragged her butt to the park to run on her own.

Waiting until after dinner meant the sun was less threatening, but the air was still hot and muggy. She started walking at a fast pace, loving the sound of the gravel under the sole of her running shoes. She wore baggy grey running shorts and a loose blue dry fit T-shirt. Most of her hair was tied back in a ponytail and a hair band was holding shorter hair off her forehead. She was already sweating from the heat alone, but Sheryl Crow sang "Run, Baby, Run" through her ear buds as she did at the beginning of every session and CC obeyed.

The fifth week of training had them doing six intervals or one minute of walking and four minutes of running. They ran more than they walked now, a feat CC still had a hard time believing. Every week they'd run a little more, and every week CC had thought she would certainly die if she ran one more second, yet she'd always found a way to keep up with the training schedule. She liked the changes she saw in her body. Her legs were developing muscles. Her butt was getting firmer and sat slightly higher, rounder. Her posture was straighter and taller. She already liked what she saw in the mirror a lot more, but surprisingly enough the physical changes were not the ones she appreciated the most. She had more energy, more confidence, more pride. Her relationship with Liz was certainly a big help in that department, but she knew exercise played a big role as well. When she focused on her breathing as she ran, she let go of all her frustrations with asshole Jeff from work, all of her rage against Liz's grandfather, all of her doubts and fears about how deeply it had affected Liz and how it might disturb their relationship. Negative thoughts and energy drained through her pores, along with abundant sweat, and all she was left with was the good stuff. A job she enjoyed, a good friend in Kayla, a great boss in Beth, supportive parents and a loving relationship with a woman so beautiful, talented and smart that tears welled up in her eyes every time she stopped to think how lucky she was to have Liz in her life.

Since the first night they'd made love after Liz's very emotional revelation, their connection had deepened. Liz had spent several nights with CC. They worked out, made dinner, chatted, watched a little TV or read as they cuddled on the couch, made love and fell asleep in each other's arms. It was very comforting, sweet and natural, and CC was rapidly growing accustomed to it all.

If only she could get rid of that annoying gut feeling that the other shoe would eventually drop. As much as she ran and filled her brain and soul with positive thoughts and feelings, that irritating concern was the one thing she could never completely get out of her mind.

She heard the beep of her watch signaling the end of her second four-minute-long run and slowed her pace down to a fast walk. She focused on her breathing, knowing the one minute she had to recuperate would pass way too fast. She always kept her music at a volume that was low enough to allow her to remain aware of her surroundings, so as Cyndi Lauper sang about girls wanting to have fun she still heard steps coming fast behind her. She first recognized the large dog that ran past her, then the perfect ass of the woman running with the animal. They were the same duo CC and Liz had seen the day they had a picnic in the park, the same duo that had inspired them to start running too. CC was surprised when the woman slowed down a few feet in front of her, much to the dog's chagrin, judging by the way he pulled on the leash. CC soon caught up with them, and as she walked past them she was so fixated on the dog that the woman's voice startled her. "Hey there."

CC was even more shocked when she realized the voice, the perfect ass and the humongous dog all belonged to Beth. "Oh, hi. I didn't expect to see you here."

"Obviously," Beth said chuckling. "Time to run again?" she asked when she heard CC's watch beep.

"Yep."

"All right, let's go," she teased as she started running, clearly slowing down her usual pace to run with CC. The dog seemed happier now that he was running, but he still pulled slightly on the leash, confirming that CC's speed wasn't the one they were used to. CC stared at him as they ran in silence, grateful that Beth didn't expect her to keep a conversation going while running. The dog wasn't that tall, but his wide chest and his big, square head and intimidating underbite made him appear more imposing. His short mahogany coat showed all of his muscles, and that dog was definitely all muscles. They slowed down to walk after four minutes. CC was busy catching her breath when Beth asked, "Where's Liz? I thought you did this running thing together."

"We do," CC managed to answer between quick and short air intakes. "But it was too hot for her today."

"Oh, I understand. I usually run during my lunch break, but today was way too hot for us too."

"Really? Lunch? You have enough time?"

Beth seemed amused by the great difficulty with which CC had delivered these few words. "Yeah, I live right on the edge of the park, so it's easy for me to go for my half-hour run, take a quick shower, and then get right back to work. Plus it gives me a chance to let the dog out."

"Wow, I…"

"I know, another thing you didn't know about me right?" Beth winked at CC and started running when CC's watch beeped again. *Damn watch*, CC thought before she followed. This was her fourth running interval. For some reason the running interval in the middle of a session was always the most difficult, the one she had to fight so hard not to quit. Focusing on the dog running slightly in front of her helped this time. She noticed the large white feet of the animal, contrasting with the rusty brown of his coat, and the way they hit the gravel under them. She also noticed when Beth increased her speed almost imperceptibly toward the end of the interval: she decided to push herself and follow. Fortunately her watch beeped shortly after she made that silly decision. She thought she would pass out for sure.

"Breathe out, Ciel. Let all the air out before you breathe in again," Beth said, placing her hand on CC's back as if she could help her push the air out of her lungs. Somehow it worked. With Beth's hand on her back and her voice gently prompting, "Air in…air out," CC regulated her breathing and recuperated much faster than usual.

They used the same technique for the last two intervals, and as they finally cooled down with a slower walk CC felt really, really good. She'd made so much progress in one single workout session with Beth and her dog. "Thank you," she told Beth sincerely, glowing in the serenity she had experienced to a certain degree after every run but never as completely as today.

"You're most welcome," Beth said. Both of her eyes remained closed for a second before she opened them again. "That was fun."

"It was." CC watched as Beth got a water bottle from the belt around her waist and took a sip before pouring some in the palm of her hand for her dog. The dog drank, and they resumed walking. The dog was now walking between them, his tongue hanging out, content. For the first time CC dared patting him on the head in a clumsy but affectionate touch. "So what kind of dog is he?"

"She."

"Oh, sorry," CC said to the dog with genuine contrition, making Beth giggle.

"It's all right. I don't think she noticed. And to answer your question, she's a Boxer. And her name is Willow."

"Cool name," CC said with a smile. "Same name as my favorite character on…"

"*Buffy the Vampire Slayer*," Beth completed to CC's surprise. "My favorite too. I have all the DVDs. That's where this one got her name. Willow's so badass." They laughed, and CC was truly sad to see that they'd reached the parking lot and were approaching her Jetta. "Well, I really did have fun this evening, Ciel. If you ever need a running partner again, let me know, okay?"

"Sure." Beth's voice had been softer than her typical tone, and CC didn't know how to interpret it. She looked into her eyes for a clue and couldn't help the words that escaped her mouth next. "Wow, I'd never noticed your eyes were so…green."

"I know. It's the exercise. Yours have never been so blue. Good night, Ciel." And with that she was gone, running with Willow as CC watched with a grin on her face she couldn't quite explain.

* * *

When CC arrived at the loft, she was pleased to find Liz lounging on the couch with the biography of Georgia O'Keefe CC had given her to celebrate their first month anniversary. She was wearing silky chocolate pajama bottoms and a white tank top. No bra, CC noticed. CC was sweaty, sticky and most

likely smelly so she didn't cozy up to Liz on the couch as she desperately wanted to but simply placed a quick kiss on top of the red hair.

"Hey there, beautiful. You'll never guess who I ran into in the park." She started walking away from Liz and toward the kitchen sink to get water, but she'd not completed her first step when Liz grabbed her hand to stop her. She looked up from her book with a suggestive grin.

"Where do you think you're going, sexy thing? Come here and kiss me properly."

CC let Liz pull her onto her lap as she protested without conviction. "Stop Liz. Seriously, I stink."

"I don't care. You're always so hot after a run. In every possible way." She took CC's face between her hands and kissed her mouth thoroughly, leaving CC even thirstier. "Mm, that's better. Now tell me who you ran into in the park."

"Oh right," CC said, hesitating for a moment after Liz's kiss temporarily erased any memory of her encounter with Beth. "Remember the woman we saw running with her dog when we had our picnic?"

"The one with an ass to die for?" At CC's instant heat on her face, Liz added, "Oh come on, don't tell me you didn't notice."

"I don't know. I don't remember," she lied. "Anyway, it turns out it was my boss, Beth."

"Oh great," Liz said with cutting sarcasm that shocked CC. The lust and playfulness that were in Liz's eyes a moment earlier completely disappeared. She didn't push CC off her lap but might as well have, the way she picked up her book from where it'd fallen onto the couch and redirected her gaze to its pages, making it clear CC was no longer wanted. Her tone was tainted with disdain when she asked, "So did you run together?"

"Well, yeah."

"Great," she said again, punctuating the word with an irritated huff. CC stood up and went to the kitchen to get the glass of water she wanted. She drank it all right there in the kitchen, standing in front of the sink and wondering what was the cause of Liz's reaction. When she went back to the living

room, Liz was still acting as if her book was the most interesting thing in the room.

CC sat at the other end of the couch in silence, torn between expressing how truly annoyed she was with Liz's unjustified reaction and simply asking her what was bothering her. She took a deep breath and chose the grown-up option, as always. "What's wrong, Liz?"

CC didn't have to wait long for an answer. She jumped, startled by the noise the heavy book made when it hit the coffee table after Liz abruptly threw it away. The redhead then turned on the couch to face CC with anger screaming all over her face.

"What's wrong is I don't see how you think it's okay for you to run with a woman who obviously hates my guts. It's bad enough you have to work with the bitch. Now you have to run with her too? Why don't you fucking date her while you're at it, CC? Better yet, go ahead and fuck her brains out!" Liz got up and stormed out of the room before CC could respond.

CC jumped again when Liz slammed the bedroom door. *What the hell.* She went to the kitchen for another glass of water which she drank very slowly, trying to cool the heat that was growing within her and that she barely recognized. Her own anger. Even Jeff Hudson had never made her blood boil this way. *What in the fucking hell.* Liz was jealous? But why? She'd never talked about Beth in any way that could indicate she had any interest in her. She barely ever talked about her at all. Hell until recently she had never even noticed the woman had a nice body, and she certainly hadn't shared that discovery with her girlfriend. Liz was definitely pushing CC's limits with her irrational bullshit. *That's right, bullshit.* She was so tempted to explode in Liz's face and shout the word: bullshit! Instead she calmly walked to the bedroom and sat on the bed where Liz lay on her stomach, her face in a pillow and her hands tightly closed into fists on either side of her head. Like a four-year-old in the middle of a tantrum.

"Baby," CC started. She rarely used terms of endearment, unlike Liz who seemed to find a new one every day, but "baby" seemed appropriate at the time. "First of all, I don't know why you think Beth hates you, but she doesn't even know you so I really doubt that's the case."

"She didn't want me to talk to you that day, keeping me out of her precious little QA room."

CC breathed in and out. *That again.* "That wasn't about you, Liz. No rep is allowed in the QA room." She stopped short of adding, "I already told you that." She knew that would get her nowhere. Instead she dared to place her hand on Liz's lower back and started a slow and soothing circular motion. Liz kept her face in the pillow, but CC noticed her hands relax ever so slightly.

"Second of all, I didn't plan on running with Beth this evening. She was there, that's all. I would've preferred running with you. You're my running partner, the best running partner and the only running partner I want." That part was only half true, but now was not the time for nuances. Liz turned to her side, and CC was amazed at the sight of a large wet spot on the pillow. How Liz had managed to cry so many tears in so little time and over such a non-issue was puzzling to say the least. She wiped the tears off one of Liz's exposed cheeks and was rewarded with a hint of a smile.

"Really?" Liz's voice was as soft as it had been harsh a few minutes ago. CC couldn't help but smile at the sudden vulnerability.

"Of course. Why on earth would you ever be jealous of Beth? I really don't get it. Have I ever said anything to make you feel that way?"

Liz covered the hand that was still resting on her cheek with her own and kissed the palm tenderly. "Beth's hot for you, baby doll. You've got to know that right?"

"What? That's ridiculous."

"I'm not making it up, CC. Everyone in the office talks about it. Are you fucking blind?"

CC was taken aback by Liz's declaration. As far as she knew Beth was straight, but even if she wasn't and even if she did have feelings for CC, which was extremely unlikely, she would never admit such feelings to anyone in the office. Beth was as secretive as they come. CC would have been more receptive to rumors of Beth being a spy for a foreign government than any of this crap Liz was telling her. Not to mention that if there had been any talk in the office of Beth having some kind of feelings for CC, Kayla would surely have mentioned it. She hated doubting Liz's word but couldn't find a way to believe her. And she didn't understand why she was making this up.

"Well, I really don't think Beth's hot for me, as you say, but even if she was it wouldn't matter. I'm all yours, Liz. You have to believe that." She bent down to kiss Liz's cheek.

"Okay. I'll believe you for now. But I can't promise I won't need a reminder once in a while."

"I can deal with that," CC replied as she kissed Liz again, this time on the lips. She giggled when Liz sniffed at her skin loudly.

"Oh my god, you do stink," she said with a smirk that made CC laugh even more.

"I know. I'm jumping in the shower right now. Care to join me?"

"Try to stop me."

They undressed on their way to the bathroom and walked into running hot water together. CC was relieved to see Liz so playful and loving again, but she couldn't shake what had just happened as easily. Although Liz's unpredictability was one of the qualities she loved about her, sometimes the roller coaster ride was unsettling and she could not adapt to the ups and downs as quickly as she was expected to.

Right now she wasn't even in the mood to fool around, if she was honest with herself, but she feared being honest with Liz would stir another outburst. An outburst of what exactly she didn't know, but she didn't want to find out. It was much easier to let Liz soap up her body under hot water. She closed her eyes and tried to focus on the feeling of Liz's hands traveling down her back to her ass. Living in the moment had taken a whole new meaning since she started dating Liz. This was a good one and she couldn't afford to miss it. This was not the other shoe dropping.

CHAPTER TEN

On Thursday evening CC was sprawled across Kayla's and Damon's sectional, feeling uncomfortably full from the dinner they'd shared. A ridiculous number of half-empty Chinese food containers were spread all over the coffee table. Damon was stretched out on the other side of the sectional while Kayla was busy rolling a blunt, or dessert as she called it, sitting in the middle section. CC's stomach was no longer used to so much food, and she promised herself she would stay away from egg rolls, lo-mein and sweet and sour chicken for a very long time. She envied Damon's sweats and was contemplating unbuttoning her jeans when Damon turned to her with a lazy smile. "So, CC, how long are you gonna keep us waiting?"

"Waiting for what?"

"Don't play innocent, girlie. You've been fucking that woman for a couple weeks now, and we still don't know if she's a real fire crotch." Kayla snickered and the movement made weed fall out of her cigar paper so she had to start over. *That'll teach you to make fun of me*, CC thought. Yet she couldn't help but smile at their childish obsession with the color of her girlfriend's pubic hair.

"You're such an ass, Damon. I don't kiss and tell, so give it up."

"Oh, come on, CC, spill it out already." Kayla offered CC a devilish half-grin before she continued. "You know we won't drop it till you tell us. Just sayin'."

CC knew all too well that was the truth, and she didn't really see the point in keeping it from them. "All right, all right. I know you guys have been together forever and probably need to get your kick somewhere so I'll tell you. Just remember it when you start fighting the seven-year itch." She paused as she straightened up in her seat, acting like she had a very important announcement to make. "The carpet is very short and narrow, but I was still able to conclude that it definitely matches the drapes."

Kayla and Damon burst out in laughter, and CC felt compelled to do the same, loving the uncomplicated nature of their company. She was in dire need of simplicity in her life, she realized. Something she had too much of before she met Liz and never thought she could miss.

Her expression must have betrayed her deeper thoughts because Damon stopped laughing to ask, "What's wrong, CC? You don't seem all that happy to be bagging an authentic fire crotch."

"Stop with that. Really, it's offensive. And there's nothing wrong. It's just...complicated."

Damon sat up to face her and became unexpectedly serious. "Okay CC. We won't say those words again, that's settled. But you know you can talk to us right? We're friends and we're not only here to joke around. We've got your back, girl." Kayla stretched out her arm to cover Damon's hand with her own and nodded in agreement with her boyfriend.

Seeing her friends unified in such a simple, tender touch moved CC. She wondered if Kayla had ever kept anything from Damon in fear of his reaction. She had to smile to herself. Kayla would never fear anyone's reaction. She considered Damon's invitation to talk and hesitated for a brief moment, knowing Kayla already had her doubts about Liz and not wanting her friend to dislike her girlfriend even more. Her need to talk finally won over her concern.

"Well, she's gorgeous and brilliant and I love her very much. But she also has these mood swings that are very hard to keep up with. One minute she's all lovey-dovey and the next she's pissed off and slamming doors. It gets very confusing."

"I bet," Damon said with a smile, encouraging her to continue.

"I knew the bitch was crazy," Kayla added with much less tact.

CC instantly became protective of Liz and their relationship. "She's not crazy, she's just moody." She grunted with frustration before adding, "I knew I should've kept my mouth shut."

"Nonsense!" Damon interrupted. "We're your friends and we're gonna listen." He glared at Kayla with a reprimanding look CC had never before seen him use. It was not threatening, but it left no doubt that he meant business. "And we're not gonna judge, right, K?"

In that moment CC understood why her friends' relationship worked so well. Damon was undoubtedly the only person in the world who could have any kind of influence on Kayla's attitude and make her as genuinely sorry as she appeared to be now. He was her balance.

"Right, sorry, CC. Go on," Kayla offered as Damon gently squeezed her hand.

"Okay, take Monday for example. I get home after my run, and she's acting so loving, starts kissing me right away like she can't wait to have me. Then I mention I met Beth in the park and she goes off, yelling that I might as well fuck Beth if I'm going to run with her. Then she runs off and slams the bedroom door. Am I wrong thinking that was a little extreme? I had no idea what was going on."

"Shit, that's *very* extreme, I'd say. Does that kind of stuff happen a lot?" Damon asked.

"All the time. She goes from ecstatic to crying her eyes out in half the time it takes me to blink and I'm left in the dust wondering what the fuck is going on." CC shrugged and shook her head to demonstrate the state of confusion she was describing. Then she looked at Kayla, who was about to light the blunt. "You're too quiet over there. You can still tell me what you're thinking, K. I need to hear it."

Kayla took a hit of the blunt and handed it to Damon before she finally opened her mouth to speak.

"Okay, I'm not gonna say the ups and downs are not cr— weird," she caught herself. Although CC was not certain why "weird" was better than "crazy." "Because they're fucking weird, no doubt. And you shouldn't have to put up with that shit. But about Beth…" Kayla interrupted her thought to take another hit of the blunt Damon had handed back to her. She held the smoke in.

CC was in no mood to wait. "What about Beth? Spill it out, K."

She finally let the smoke out. "Well, you can't blame the girl for being jealous, CC."

"What? Why?" CC was losing her patience.

"You're kidding me right? Are you really gonna sit there and tell me you don't know boss bitch would die to eat that disgusting yogurt she brings you off your body?"

"What? Where the hell is that coming from? Is everyone in the office really thinking that, like Liz said? And if that's the case, why haven't you told me about it before?"

"I was sure you knew, baby girl. I figured you were just not interested."

"Well, I didn't know, K. I didn't know because it's not true. Beth has never come on to me. I don't even think she's gay, for Christ's sake! And I hope to God the rumors didn't come from you because that would really, really piss me off." She thought the veins in her head would explode from the burning pressure she felt inside it.

"Whoa, missy! Calm the fuck down. The rumors were running wild long before I started in QA. If anything, my being there helped 'cuz before I was in QA everyone thought the two of you were munching on each other all day long in that little room of yours. I'm the one who keeps telling them I've never seen anything juicy going on."

CC sighed with frustration. "What the hell is wrong with these people?"

"They're bored, CC. They'll take any piece of crap they're given and blow it out of proportion. That's what they do. And in this case they had more than crap. Beth brings you coffee every morning, she looks at you like your shit don't stink and she praises you any chance she gets. Plus you spent all that time alone and everyone knows you're officially a dyke."

CC bent forward and grabbed her head with both hands, her elbows resting on her knees. "I can't believe you never told me about this. Of all the things you could have kept quiet about."

"I'm sorry, CC. I was sure you knew. Plus I didn't want trouble with Beth. The woman has a stick up her ass half the time, but she treats me well and I have mad respect for her. Not her fault she's in love with you. Hell, if I played for your team I'd want a piece of that too. Especially now that you started that running bullshit. I mean, have you looked at your ass lately? "

"Oh shut up. She's not in love with me. Let's drop it okay?"

"Deal. Please try to relax okay? I didn't mean to upset you. Here, take a hit of this." Kayla held the blunt in front of CC's face, but CC waived her hand to refuse the offer.

"No thanks."

Kayla gave the marijuana cigar to Damon as she addressed CC. "Sorry, I figured you might take up a little weed again since Carrot-Bitch is back on nicotine."

"What?" CC felt the pressure that had barely started to subside rise up again. "Have you seen her smoke or is that just another rumor?"

"She's been out during regular smoking breaks all week, CC. Everyone's seen her. I swear I'm not shitting you. You didn't know? For real? Doesn't she smoke when she's with you?"

CC snorted a laugh. "No, she sure doesn't. As a matter of fact we were sitting on the couch yesterday talking about how good we've been feeling since we quit smoking. No wonder she doesn't want to run anymore. For Christ's sake! Now not only is she moody, but she's also a liar. What the fuck am I going to do?"

"Dump the bitch. You don't need that," was Kayla's immediate answer.

"Wait a minute," Damon interjected. "We've all done things we're not proud of. She's probably really scared you'll be disappointed in her. If you love her, CC, give the girl a chance to explain." Kayla grunted and huffed in disagreement but didn't add a word.

"You're right, Damon. I'll talk to her," CC said as she stretched her arm forward. "Now give me that." Damon gave CC the blunt while Kayla snickered. CC inhaled and coughed up all of the smoke on her first try, something her hosts found quite amusing, judging by their carefree laugher. She was able to keep the smoke in longer on the second try, and after the third hit she let herself fall back into her seat and enjoyed the buzz.

* * *

On Friday morning CC woke up with the worst case of cotton mouth she'd ever experienced. She needed water, a toothbrush and toothpaste. Right now and in that order. She'd fallen asleep on Kayla's and Damon's sectional the night before and when she finally made it home she found Liz asleep in her bed. CC started work an hour earlier than Liz, so even when Liz spent the night at the loft they always drove to work separately. CC often left the house before Liz was even awake. She was hoping that would be the case this morning as she slowly inched her way toward the edge of the bed. She was in no mood for a confrontation. She cringed when Liz's caustic tone stopped her progress.

"Where were you last night?" CC sighed heavily. So much for an easy escape.

"I told you I was having dinner with Kayla and her boyfriend."

"That late? It was past midnight when I fell asleep waiting for you, CC. Tell me the truth. Were you with Beth?"

"No Liz. I wasn't with Beth. That's ridiculous. I was exactly where I told you I'd be. I'm not fucking lying to you." CC quickly moved from under the sheets and a whiff of marijuana escaped from the T-shirt she'd worn to bed, the same she'd worn to Kayla's. For a second she hoped the smell didn't reach Liz, but then realized she couldn't cover up her own temporary relapse if she was going to confront Liz about smoking cigarettes. She decided the brief internal debate was obviously moot as Liz got closer to her T-shirt and took a deep breath.

"Oh my fucking god. You reek of pot!"

"That's right. I smoked a blunt with Kayla and Damon last night. It's not the end of the world." CC could barely recognize her own voice, its tone almost matching Liz's nastiness.

"Oh, it's not the end of the world, is it? We had a deal, CC. How am I supposed to trust you if you're going to do things like that behind my back?"

CC was so astounded she didn't know if she should cry or laugh. Before she could make a decision she was out of bed and had already started shouting at Liz.

"Are you fucking kidding me right now? Did you really say that? You've got some nerves, Liz McLeary. Yes, I smoked a blunt last night, but I just told you about it. Meanwhile you've been smoking all week at work and acting like you're so happy you quit when you're with me. Are you really going to sit there in my bed and lecture me on breaking deals and going behind your back? What the fuck is wrong with you? Who are you?"

Liz looked startled for a moment, then she started crying and ran to the bathroom. CC heard the door slam, but she didn't care. Liz had no right to be angry. CC was the one who should be fuming right now. And she was. Yelling hadn't exactly helped her mouth situation so she took a gulp out of the warm, half-empty water bottle she found on her dresser. She started pacing back and forth in front of the bed, trying to answer her own question. Who was she really dating? How could Liz sit on her high horse and accuse her of keeping secrets when she was the one lying through her teeth? It was so manipulative, so dishonest, so…evil. *Dump the bitch*, she heard Kayla's voice say to her.

She started making the bed. She might as well do something useful since she couldn't keep still, yet somehow couldn't seem to leave the bedroom either. She took care of her own side first and then moved to what had become Liz's side. She cussed when she set her bare foot on a hard and cold piece of metal and when she looked down she realized it was the spiral binding of Liz's notebook. She picked up the notebook and distractedly glanced at the page to which it was open before she threw it nonchalantly onto the bedside table. Something caught her eye so she looked again. *God, the bitch has talent.*

CC sat on the bed and grabbed the notebook to get a better look at Liz's art. What she saw as she turned the pages was a series of small sketches. She knew Liz would keep sketching in the pages of her notebook until she was satisfied with the results and would then move her ideas to a larger canvas. She'd been playing with pointillism, using dots to create shapes, light and shadows. Page after page CC studied variations of ruffled sheets covering curves that were not quite identifiable yet distinctively feminine. She recognized her own sheets, white cotton with sateen stripes. How Liz was able to show the texture and softness of the sateen stripes with simple dots was mystifying. CC figured the feminine curves must have been hers, or Liz's, or both of their bodies intertwined. Each sketch revealed a word barely outlined by faded dots in the middle of the ruffled sheets. A few said "love," which touched CC. One said "lover," which made her smile. But the one she preferred simply spelled "home." CC could only imagine what the penciled sketches she was observing might look like on a larger scale. The thought took her breath away.

God, I love the bitch, she reminded herself as she reveled in Liz's art and talent. She was such a special, unique woman. Who cared if she smoked? And who cared if she was moody? History showed artists weren't always the easiest people to live with, but being part of their universe was worth the pain, wasn't it? She was already halfway convinced when Liz sat carefully beside her on the bed and rested her head on her shoulder.

"Do you like them?" she asked timidly.

"I love them, Liz. They're really beautiful."

"They're us, CC." She raised her head to look at CC and rolled her eyes. "Well, they're not us this morning, but that's my fault, isn't it? I'm so sorry, CC. I fucked up."

She started crying again, and CC let the notebook fall onto the bed so she could pull her into her arms. Her T-shirt was soon wet with tears and she could barely understand what Liz was saying against her chest.

"I should've told you I started smoking again, but I was so scared you'd hate me for it. I mean, it was my idea to quit. I know that. I must be such a huge disappointment to you. I'd understand if you had enough of me. Really."

Liz's tendency to overdramatize everything sometimes made CC smile; this was one of those instances. Mostly because it made her see that her own reaction might also have been slightly over the top.

"I'm not going to leave you over a few cigarettes, baby. I just wish you would've told me about it. Whether you smoke or not is you choice. But don't hide it from me. That's what pissed me off."

"I know, I know. I'm so stupid. I fuck up everything."

"Shh. Stop it. It's over now. So we've established that you're a smoker. At least for the time being. That's all there is to it. Okay?" CC started worrying when Liz broke their embrace to look at her with a sheepish pout on her face.

"Well, actually there's something else."

CC bunched up a part of the sheets into her fists as she braced herself for whatever it was Liz wanted to add to their already eventful morning. "Okay. What is it?"

"I don't want to run anymore. It's boring and I hate it."

CC couldn't help but laugh as she relaxed again. "Okay, baby. I'm not going to make you run, don't worry. I can keep doing it on my own."

Liz sighed heavily with relief, as if she'd been holding her breath for their entire conversation. "Are you sure? You're not mad at me?"

"No, I'm not mad. But I do have to jump in the shower now or I'll be late." CC quickly kissed Liz's forehead and stood up to start walking to the bathroom. Liz grabbed her hands to stop her and held them in her own, looking up at her with tender green eyes.

"Thank you for forgiving me, cupcake. I'm really sorry I lied and I promise I'll make it up to you. Tonight. I'll cook for you, I'll feed you and then…"

Liz's eyes sparkled and darkened all at once, a phenomenon CC would never grow tired of. She smiled and raised one eyebrow in question. "And then what?"

Liz's voice was low and inviting when she answered, "I can't tell you, but I'll give you a clue." She lowered CC's panties just enough to kiss the sensitive mound of flesh where soft curls should have been but that CC preferred to keep shaved. The kiss was long and thorough as Liz's tongue followed the same path as her lips and ended with a gentle bite. CC was about to beg her to move lower, where the same flesh parted into labium, but Liz moved her panties back up and sent her to the shower with a light slap on the butt.

"Tonight lover. Tonight," she said with a smile as frustrating as it was seductive.

* * *

"So that's it? All is forgiven? Just like that?" Kayla asked as she held her morning marijuana cigar in front of CC, who waved it off as she merged onto I-87 South.

"No thanks. I have a feeling I'll regret last night's buzz enough as it is when I go running after work." CC had already decided that the fact Liz had gone back to smoking and had quit running didn't mean she had to do the same. She enjoyed her new habits. They made her feel better about herself and the fact they hadn't been her idea in the beginning didn't mean she had to reject them now. And the fact Kayla thought she should break up with Liz didn't mean she had to either.

"Yes, just like that, K. She's a smoker. So what? You smoke weed and you have a big mouth, but I still like you, don't I?" She grinned at Kayla, hoping she would let it go. No such luck.

"All right. So let's say you forgive the lies about smoking. I get that. It's not that big a deal, for real. But what about her moody crap? Are you really gonna keep putting up with that shit?"

"Yes. I guess I am. She's worth it."

Kayla blew out her last hit with exasperation as she put the blunt away. They were still two miles from the D&B office. "You're a sucker, you know that right? Just sayin'."

"Okay, I'm a sucker." CC was annoyed with Kayla's insistence. "Come on, K. No couple is perfect. I needed to talk last night and I appreciated you listening and even giving me your opinion, but in the end it's my choice. Do I tell you to leave Damon every time you tell me he's being an asshole? Which is pretty much every other day?"

Kayla wanted to laugh but fought it so only a half grin showed when she answered CC. "No, I guess you don't."

"That's right. I don't. I was mad at Liz last night, but we're okay now and I still want to be with her. Can you respect that? Or do I have to keep the next fight to myself?"

"I can respect that, CC. Because you're asking me. But I swear if she hurts you real bad in the end I'll fuck her up."

CC chuckled at the thought. "No, you won't. You'll just be there for me." They smiled at each other in agreement as CC pulled into the parking lot of the office building at the same time as Beth. They were a few minutes late. CC got out of the car and went to help Beth when she saw her struggling with the expected two coffees but more bags than usual. Kayla lit up a cigarette meanwhile, oblivious to Beth's need for help.

"Good morning," CC said as she took one bag and one coffee from Beth's hands.

"Good morning, and thank you," Beth answered with a smile before turning to Kayla. "Here's your bagel. Take it now so you don't have to come to the QA room after you smoke your cigarette and then have to go back to the breakroom. It'll save you a few steps." If Kayla noticed the same hint of sarcasm CC did in Beth's voice, she didn't seem embarrassed by it in the least.

"Thank you, boss. See you in a few," she simply said as she took the brown paper bag Beth was offering.

CC saw Beth roll her eyes as they walked to the building door together, and she winked at her. "On the bright side, maybe this way she won't need another smoking break before nine." Beth giggled and let CC open the door for her.

"Thank you, that's so kind of you."

"Oh, please, it's the least I could do. Especially since I have a feeling you'll share whatever's in these bags with me." CC followed Beth into the breakroom.

"Very perceptive of you. I tried a new recipe for dinner last night and I made way too much. I thought we could share it for lunch. It's some kind of healthy version of tuna casserole. Not bad at all."

"That sounds yummy, but won't you be going for your run at lunch?"

"Nah," Beth said as she placed their lunch in the refrigerator. "It's going to be a hot one again. I'll go after dinner. Would you care to join me and Willow?"

CC noted a twinkle in Beth's eyes as she made the invitation. "Oh, I would love to, but I can't. I'm going to run right after work today because I have plans for dinner." The twinkle was replaced with obvious disappointment, and CC couldn't help but think of the rumors she'd learned about the night before. Was it possible Beth really was interested in her?

"Of course you do. Silly me. It's Friday after all. You're probably having dinner with Liz." Beth closed the refrigerator door and exited the breakroom to make her way to the QA room, followed closely by CC, who decided to test the waters a little.

"That's right. But what about you? No hot date with your boyfriend?"

She didn't know what she'd expected, but it was certainly not the hurt she saw in Beth's eyes. Her smile was not returned. In fact, Beth's inflection was polite but cold when she answered. "I'm not dating anyone, Ciel. But if I were, it wouldn't be a man." Without giving CC a chance to respond Beth disappeared into her cubicle.

When CC approached to grab a yogurt and fruit, Beth didn't turn from her computer screen. "I'm sorry if I offended you, Beth. I didn't know. You never told me."

Beth looked at her over her shoulder and offered a weak smile. "I know. Don't worry about it, Ciel. Maybe I should have told you before." She quickly turned back to her computer, but CC could have sworn her eyes glimmered with tears.

* * *

CC got out of the shower and dressed in a pair of faded denim shorts and a dark blue tank top. She'd completed her last training session of Week Five with success. Next week she would be running five-minute intervals and she was excited about it. In a month she would be expected to run thirty minutes nonstop. Even though the accomplishment now seemed possible, the thought still left her with some apprehension, so she put it aside to focus on the delicious aromas coming from her kitchen and the Tori Amos music Liz was singing along to. Liz was decidedly in a good mood this evening. She'd kept her promise to cook dinner, and her demeanor had been nothing but inviting and alluring since CC made it home.

CC showed up in the kitchen singing along to "Precious Things" which made Liz laugh. At first CC hadn't been a big fan of Liz's idol. She thought her music was strange and quite depressing. Soon, however, she found herself buying her own copy of *Little Earthquakes*. She played it in the car all the time, much to Kayla's chagrin. The artist had grown on CC. There was a certain darkness about her work, perhaps, but it was paired with musical genius. CC had also discovered a wonderful sense of sarcasm in the artist that she enjoyed immensely. And in the end she was grateful to Liz for introducing her to Ms. Amos's music.

When Liz looked away from her to concentrate on the recipe that was sitting on the countertop, CC stopped to take in the sight. Liz was standing in front of the stove wearing a green camisole that was almost entirely hidden behind her black apron, which CC found extremely sexy. Her hair was up in a messy bun, and she mumbled words to herself as she measured ingredients. She was so lovely. CC couldn't resist walking behind Liz and letting her arms snake around her waist as she kissed the neck left exposed by her hairdo. "What are we having? It smells wonderful."

"Tangerine and rosemary duck salad. Want a taste?"

"Of course."

Liz took a spoon and filled it with the sauce she'd been working on before bringing it inches from CC's lips with a mischievous grin. When CC moved closer to the spoon, Liz quickly turned it to her own mouth and emptied it of its content, purposefully leaving her lips coated with the sauce. "Well, what are you waiting for?"

Completely seduced by the playfulness, CC slowly licked each of Liz's lips before deepening the kiss, humming her pleasure as she relished the sweet and savory taste. "Delicious," she whispered.

Liz's voice became lower and lost its humor when she spoke again. "Glad you like it. It goes very well with this merlot." She took a large gulp of the red wine she'd been drinking while cooking and kissed CC more aggressively. CC's mouth was flooded with the taste of the wine, and she groaned as Liz's tongue became more invasive. She let Liz back her into the kitchen island and loved the pressure of Liz's thigh between her legs. She was starting to think they should skip dinner when she heard the buzzing of the intercom. Startled, Liz jumped backward and shouted, "What the hell? I fucking hate that thing! It scared me half to death."

CC laughed at Liz's panicked expression. "Sounds like we have visitors, baby. And I have a pretty good idea who they are."

"No, not your parents. Are you serious? I look like shit, CC."

"You look gorgeous, as always," CC said as she placed a kiss on Liz's cheek. She went to the intercom to let her parents in. "Come on up, guys."

CC was not quite as surprised by their unannounced visit as Liz appeared to be. She had only herself to blame. She knew how delighted they were that she was dating someone and how anxious they were to meet Liz. She also knew that sooner or later they would grow tired of waiting and drop by hoping Liz would be there, as she was this evening. She turned back to Liz and found her frozen in front of the stove with a terror-stricken look on her face. She immediately ran back to her to try to put her at ease.

"It'll be okay. I promise. They'll love you. Take a deep breath," she said as she rubbed Liz's arms. Liz obeyed, but her smile was tentative at best when she let her breath out. She removed her apron when they heard a knock on the door. CC took her hand, and they went to answer together.

"Hi, honey, I hope we're not bothering you, but we missed you too much," Marie said as she entered the loft and hugged her daughter.

"You're not bothering us, Mom. We were just about to have dinner. Hi Dad," CC added as she hugged her father next.

"Hey baby."

"There's plenty of food for all of us. I hope you'll stay and join us." The polite invitation came from Liz. To CC, her voice seemed flat, empty of real emotion, but she doubted her parents would notice, and if they did they would blame it on nerves as CC was trying to do.

"Mom, Dad, meet Liz McLeary, my girlfriend."

Liz courteously extended her hand, but Marie pulled her into a warm hug. "Liz! It's so good to finally meet you." She released Liz from their embrace but kept holding her at arm's length. "Look at you! You're just as beautiful as Ciel told us you were."

"You sure are. Nice to meet you, young lady." Charles hugged Liz in his turn, albeit with more reserve.

"Thank you. It's very nice to meet you too, Mr. and Mrs. Charbonneau," Liz answered formally with a smile that bore little resemblance to her familiar, warmer smile. She'd expected Liz to be nervous the first time she would meet her parents, but she wasn't prepared for that level of discomfort. It was almost as if Liz had checked out to be replaced with a perfect little Stepford wife.

"Oh, please call us Marie and Charles," CC heard her father say.

"Yes, please. We like to think we're younger than we really are," Marie added with a joyous giggle.

"Oh no, I'm sorry, I didn't mean…"

"We know you didn't, Liz. I'm joking." Marie smiled at Liz before moving on to the living room.

CC placed her hand on Liz's back in an attempt to relax her while her parents walked closer to the painting Liz had given her on their first date. She'd finally hung it above the couch a couple of weeks ago and wasn't surprised when her parents were drawn to it.

"I knew they'd love you," she whispered to Liz's ear. Her hand and her words weren't enough to appease Liz, who was still tense when they joined CC's parents in front of the artwork. "I told you she had talent," CC told Marie and Charles, her hand still on the small of Liz's back.

"You were right. I have no words for how beautiful this is, Liz." CC finally felt the muscles on Liz's back relax a little and recognized a genuine smile as she took in Marie's praise. "The way you play with the light and shadows and explore so many hues of blue is amazing. CC already told us her eyes were your inspiration, but I think I would have recognized my daughter's very soul in that painting even if I hadn't known. You're quite the artist, my dear."

Liz loosened up and leaned into CC while she listened to the laudatory description of her art. When Marie stopped talking and looked at her with a tender, motherly smile, Liz walked to her and hugged her with the abandon she'd been incapable of a few minutes earlier.

"Thank you. It means so much to hear you say this, Mrs.— Marie," she caught herself. "You're too kind. Now I know where CC got that beautiful heart of hers."

They all laughed, and CC was relieved to see Liz's eyes sparkle again. She wanted her parents to meet the real Liz, the one she'd fallen in love with, and they just had.

They chatted for a while about Liz's painting and her new interest in pointillism. Marie and Charles both shared a real interest in art so the conversation seemed to enchant them. CC observed, pleased yet puzzled with how quickly and drastically Liz's disposition had changed. She was too busy analyzing the situation to be a good host and was abruptly brought back to reality when Liz asked their guests, "Would you like some wine?" Marie and Charles both accepted the offer.

"I'll help you," CC said before following Liz into the open concept kitchen. "Are you okay now?" she whispered as Liz poured four glasses of wine.

"Yes. Your parents are great, darling. You're very lucky."

"I know. And I'm glad you think so too." Liz gave her a quick peck on the lips and walked back to the living room with two glasses of wine. CC followed with two more, offering one to her father and keeping the other.

When Liz attempted to hand one of her glasses to Marie, she let it go too quickly and some of the red wine spilled onto Marie's cream-colored blouse. CC's mother let out a small yelp from the shock and then immediately started laughing. Liz looked like she was going to cry when she said, "Oh my god, I thought you had it. I'm so sorry."

"Don't worry about it, dear. It's just an old blouse I won't even miss," Marie said to dismiss the incident, taking a sip of the wine that remained in the glass she was now holding.

But Liz wouldn't let it go. "But it's such a beautiful blouse. I'm a clumsy idiot," she admonished herself before tears started running down her cheeks. "Damn idiot," she added harshly before running to the bathroom. She was gone for a long time during which CC and her parents looked at each other without saying a word, wondering what was going on. When Liz came back with a wet washcloth for Marie, her face was still marked with tears and anguish. Marie took the washcloth and rubbed a bit at the wine without much conviction. They all knew the blouse was ruined.

"I'll give you one of my T-shirts, Mom. I don't think we'll save this old blouse."

"Thank you, honey."

"I'm so sorry, Mrs. Charbonneau. Tell me where you bought it, please. I'll buy you a new one. I can't believe I was so stupid."

Marie put her hands on Liz's shoulders and forced the younger woman to hold her gaze. "Liz, dear, look at me. I know you're upset and I understand why, but it was an accident and you have to let it go now. Okay? You hear me?"

Liz nodded sheepishly, and CC went to the bedroom to grab a T-shirt for her mother. She felt a tightening in her chest. The tone her mother had used with Liz was the same she'd heard her use with patients over the phone on many occasions when their family dinners had been interrupted by one crisis or another when she was growing up. Marie changed into a clean shirt, and they sat at the table to share dinner.

The evening was pleasant enough, but CC knew something in her mother had shifted. She was in work mode, observing and analyzing Liz, probably coming up with a diagnosis. It worried CC. More than Kayla's, Beth's or even her own doubts and fears about Liz's behavior, the fact that her mother was now regarding her as a potential case made her gut flutter with anxiety.

CHAPTER ELEVEN

CC and Liz followed the rest of their group onto the *Lac du Saint-Sacrement* ship. Thanks to an abundance of windows, the three decks of the ship offered beautiful views of the lake and the Adirondack Mountains surrounding it. CC and Liz joined their coworkers in the bow of the first deck, where they found a bar and an impressive buffet. The back part of the first deck presented a central wooden dance floor flanked by carpeted areas where tables and chairs would allow guests to dine while admiring the beautiful panorama out the windows. The bow and the back were separated by an elegant staircase that led to the second deck. CC followed Liz to the bar, where they ordered beer.

"Come sit with us," Kayla said as she approached the bar at the same time as the couple.

"Sure," CC answered quickly, relieved that she would know at least one other person at their table.

"We can't, pumpkin," Liz interjected. "I already told the girls we'd sit with them," she said pointing to a group of girls CC had never had a conversation with before.

"Sorry," CC mouthed to Kayla, whose smirk did little to cover her disappointment. "I'll catch you later," she added, her tone betraying her own frustration at the turn of events as Liz grabbed her hand and pulled her away from the bar.

Dixon & Brown Communications had loaded the employees who'd signed up to attend the annual dinner cruise on a couple of buses to make the trip from Albany to Lake George. Liz, CC and Kayla were among that group.

A few others, like Beth, drove their own cars to Lake George. For the past two years, CC had driven with Beth, neither of them intending on drinking or wanting to spend more time than necessary with the account reps, who tolerated them at best. This year Liz had insisted that CC take the bus with her and CC figured her place was with her girlfriend rather than with her boss, even if she was not really in the mood to party. The highs and lows of her relationship with Liz, mostly due to Liz's own highs and lows, had only intensified in the two weeks since their dinner with CC's parents, and CC was growing tired, annoyed and sad all at once. On top of that, her luck had her sitting on the same bus as Jeff Hudson and forty-five minutes of listening to his sexist jokes and blatant flirtation with every pretty girl on the bus had pushed CC over the edge of grumpiness. *What a moron.*

CC and Liz were still walking hand in hand as they approached the table where Liz's friends were sitting when they came face to face with Beth. Beth returned CC's smile, but CC noted definite sadness behind the smile.

"Hey," CC started timidly. "How was the drive?"

"It was fine. Just seemed longer than usual. Not sure why." The sadness CC had seen in Beth's smile reached her eyes, and CC knew the simple statement was Beth's way of saying she'd missed her company. Something tugged at her heart. She had to admit she'd missed the car ride too. More than the car ride, she'd missed their arrival as a team of two against everyone else. She held Beth's gaze, trying to make her understand, and smiled more freely when she saw Beth's eyes close slowly, remaining closed for a second or two before opening up again with less sadness and more recognition.

CC had not realized she'd let go of Liz's hand until she felt that same hand grab hers again more firmly, forcing her out of her thoughts. "Good evening, Beth," she heard Liz say with a politeness that contained no sincerity.

"Liz," Beth said curtly.

CC was startled when Liz started laughing a loud, obnoxious and cold laugh. "Liz and Beth," she said before laughing again, leaving Beth and CC puzzled. "Sorry, I just realized we have the same name. Elizabeth right?"

Beth nodded in acknowledgment, still not understanding the humor in the fact that they shared a first name that was, after all, quite common.

Liz stopped laughing and continued, "I think it's funny how we have the same name, Elizabeth, but go by the opposite ends of the name. Liz and Beth. Me the top, you the bottom."

By the end of her statement Liz's tone was unmistakably antagonistic. CC witnessed the transformation of Beth's gaze from warm to glacial and braced herself for what might happen next.

"Right," Beth started with a bone-chilling smile on her mouth, "You the opening act, me the headliner." CC had a hard time not laughing at Beth's repartee until the next words killed all humor in the exchange. "But it shouldn't be surprising. Surely we all know, Liz, that you and I are opposites in most likely every possible way."

CC was surprised she didn't see a cold fog follow Beth as she disappeared into the crowd after her declaration. She was tempted to follow, but her feet wouldn't move. Her heart was heavy. She looked at the hand holding hers and couldn't muster any understanding for the hurtful banter her girlfriend had started. In that very moment she deeply disliked Liz.

"What a bitch," Liz said under her breath with a shrug before she tried to pull CC toward her friends' table.

"You started it," CC said as her feet still refused to move. "Why?"

"You know why," Liz answered, placing her hands around CC's neck and looking at her with the sweet insecurity that for the first time didn't make CC's heart melt.

"Yeah, you're jealous. So what? That doesn't give you the right to be mean to her. She hasn't done anything and I told you there's nothing between us. I tell you every day I love you and I want to be with you. *You* were the bitch, Liz. She simply defended herself."

As she said the words, CC immediately feared an outburst, but instead Liz kissed her cheek softly.

"You're right. I'm sorry. Now can we please forget it happened and try to enjoy dinner? Please?"

CC wasn't seduced by the apology but didn't want a public scene either. Plus she wasn't certain her reaction wasn't aggravated by her already grouchy mood so she followed Liz to the table. There she shared dinner with her girlfriend and women she didn't know while wondering if Beth was alone at her table and if she enjoyed the shrimp cocktail as much as they usually did. CC did not.

* * *

After dinner Liz and her friends hit the dance floor. CC excused herself, stating she needed to use the restroom. She found Beth where she expected to, standing alone outside on the third deck in the front of the boat, admiring the view in solitary silence.

"Did you enjoy dinner?" CC asked in almost a whisper, not wanting to startle Beth as she approached behind her. Beth turned to her and offered a broad smile.

"Hey there."

"Hey," CC replied, resting her hands on the rails next to Beth and letting the wind hit her face. She took a deep breath and felt like it was the first time she was really breathing since the beginning of the evening. The fresh air and the quiet soothed her.

"To be honest, no. I didn't really enjoy it. I missed your company." CC turned to see Beth looking at her, seemingly as surprised at her own candor as CC was. CC answered with a simple smile that prompted Beth to continue. "I hated these cruises before you joined QA, Ciel. The last two years had been fun with you, but tonight is just like before." Beth turned away to face the wind again and hesitated, but finally went on. "I was used to being alone back then. I never felt lonely. Tonight I feel lonely and that's what I hate the most."

CC immediately felt guilt swallow her whole. She didn't know how to express it, though, and she didn't want Beth to stop talking. She placed a comforting hand on Beth's back and felt the taller woman's muscles tense up before relaxing under the touch.

"I know we don't know much about each other, Ciel, and I can be distant and even cold, but the thing is you're the person I feel the closest to. And not just at work. I don't expect you to understand, but I guess the one thing I really want you to know about me is that your presence," she paused and turned her face to look at CC again. CC saw the tears well up in the tender eyes before Beth continued, "and your absence, affect me more than you know."

Beth's gaze was penetrating. Her face was only inches from CC's, and CC could smell a hint of wine on her breath. She'd never seen Beth drink. Was that how much her absence had affected Beth tonight? For a moment she thought Beth was going to kiss her and she panicked. She wasn't ready for a kiss or any deeper confessions from the woman she still viewed as her boss, although she had to admit she was incredibly intrigued by her, more and more every day.

She removed her hand from Beth's back, smiled and spoke in a way she hoped was light and upbeat. "Thank you. I take that as a very big compliment and I hope it's not the only thing I'll get to know about you. In fact, I think it's about time we stop just saying it and really get to know each other better. You're important to me too, Beth. I'd really like for us to be friends. So what about a run tomorrow? Me, you and Willow?"

Beth laughed and sighed at the same time. "I'd really like that. Willow too, I'm sure."

"Great. It's settled then. Let's meet at the park around nine? It's Saturday, so it'll get crowded after that."

"Not to mention hot as hell." They both laughed, and then Beth lowered her voice to almost a whisper. "Nine it is."

"Perfect," CC said with enthusiasm. She hesitated before she added, more seriously, "And I also really missed your company tonight, Beth. It wasn't the same."

In a move that shocked CC, Beth wrapped her arms around her shoulders and pulled her into a tight hug. Beth wasn't a hugger. CC had never seen her hug anyone. Still the strong arms around her were comforting, warming, and soon shock was replaced with an overall sense of exhilarating peacefulness. She let her head be cradled against Beth's shoulder and wrapped her own arms around her waist, hearing Beth gasp slightly at the returned embrace. They stayed like that, swaying together, until CC's words broke the spell.

"I'm sorry about what Liz said."

CC missed the warmth of the hug when Beth immediately pulled away and offered her a smile that was still genuine but more distant, as if CC's mention of Liz had jolted her back to reality.

"Don't worry about it. I'm sorry I said anything back. She's your girlfriend and I promise I'll show her more respect moving forward."

"You just defended yourself, Beth. She's the one who was out of line." CC reached for Beth, but Beth put more distance between them.

"Still, it put you in an awkward position and I don't want to do that ever again. Actually, you should probably go find her. She'll wonder where you are."

"But..."

"Go Ciel. I'm fine now, I promise. I'll see you tomorrow at nine."

Beth's smile was forced, but CC didn't know if she wanted to or even should protest. Beth was right. She really should be going back to her girlfriend. "Okay then. See you tomorrow." She started walking away but turned back to add, "I'm really glad we talked."

"Me too. Good night, Ciel. Have fun." CC watched Beth turn around to face the wind and wondered why she wanted to stay so badly.

* * *

CC found Liz's friends on the dance floor but no sign of Liz. Her friends mentioned she'd gone to the restroom or the bar or maybe to get some fresh air. They weren't sure but they hadn't seen her in a while. CC looked around the room and realized it was too crowded to really see anyone or anything. She looked up and recognized a familiar figure on the mezzanine of the second deck.

Joanna Dixon was standing in her favorite spot, straight and tall, her hands strongly anchored to the railing, looking down on her flock with pride. She was wearing a designer skirt power suit; CC had never seen the woman dressed for anything else than business. The suit's red fabric enhanced the dark bronze of her flawless skin, and the skirt was short enough to expose long athletic legs. Her black hair was cropped short, allowing the beauty of her strong facial features to shine, from high cheek bones to a heart-shaped mouth, as if they were sculpted to perfection. She was in her mid-forties but she looked ageless. CC had seen her standing there on each of the dinner cruises she'd attended. She was observing, assessing. She could see everything.

CC decided the best way to find Liz quickly was to imitate Joanna. She climbed the elegant staircase and walked to the mezzanine on the other side of the boat from the one where Joanna was standing, not wanting to disturb the big boss. She looked down and searched for Liz's red hair but couldn't find her anywhere. "Good evening, Ms. Charbonneau," she heard a deep female voice say behind her. "I trust you're enjoying yourself?"

CC instinctively looked to the now empty space where she'd seen Joanna stand a minute earlier to confirm the voice was hers before turning around to answer the question. "Yes, of course. Thank you for putting this together for us. We all love it." Intimidated by the woman's presence, CC turned back to look down at the crowd on the dance floor.

"Looking for someone?" Joanna asked as she stood by CC. She was a few inches shorter than CC yet somehow so imposing. "May I help?"

"I don't know if you know her. She's fairly new. Liz McLeary?"

"Oh yes, Ms. McLeary. Of course. She's one of our top performers. We'll be sad to see her go back to school in a couple of weeks." Something in CC's expression made Joanna let out a low controlled chuckle before she continued. "Don't be so surprised, Ms. Charbonneau. I know everything." Joanna's wink did nothing to weaken the meaning of her words. "I'm afraid I haven't seen Ms. McLeary in at least half an hour or so. I'm sorry."

"It's okay, thanks anyway. I'm sure she'll turn up eventually."

"That's a safe assumption. Unless she swam to shore." Joanna threw a sideways glance at CC and smirked, leaving CC no other choice but to laugh. "That's better," Joanna said before she became serious again. "Don't be so nervous, Ms. Charbonneau. You must know your work at D&B is much appreciated."

At CC's puzzled look, Joanna went on, "Ms. Andrews and I do talk, you know. She praises your work ethics every chance she gets and I value her opinion. In fact, I was hoping we'd get a chance to talk. I'd like to hear your opinion on one of our client relationship managers: Jeff Hudson."

"Oh," was all CC could manage to say, but she imagined her face couldn't hide her disdain for the man when Joanna spoke his name. Her suspicion was confirmed when Joanna laughed in the same low and controlled way she had before. CC was panic-stricken. How much could she really say about the man? Especially with the rumors circulating about him and Joanna. Her mind was spinning as she opened her mouth to talk several times without speaking a word.

"Don't let the rumors influence your words, Ms. Charbonneau. I need your honest and frank opinion on Mr. Hudson's work."

"What rumors?" CC said defensively, feeling her face flush with discomfort. She wanted to melt and let her body slip through the railing to the dance floor.

"I told you. I know everything. I don't usually address ridiculous rumors, but I'll tell you one thing. That was the last time I let Mr. Hudson borrow my car for a business lunch with a high-profile client. As I said, however, what interests me is his work performance. And that's where I want your opinion, Ms. Charbonneau."

CC sighed with relief at knowing the rumors were completely false as she'd hoped and expected and looked at Joanna straight in the eye to offer her thoughts on Jeff Hudson.

"I'm not the kind to go over anyone's head, Ms. Dixon, but since you're asking me I'll tell you exactly as I see it. Jeff Hudson's work ethics are poor. No," she corrected herself, "they're nonexistent. He sends leads through to clients that are far below their standards and expectations and completely disregards my work as a Quality Assurance representative. I think it's only a matter of time before we lose the accounts he manages, Ms. Dixon, and I'm not saying that lightly."

Joanna nodded and smiled at CC. "Thank you. I appreciate your opinion. One more thing, Ms. Charbonneau. I know you're very happy in the QA department, but would you ever consider advancement if a position, let's say for example, in client relationship management were to suddenly be made available?"

It was CC's turn to smirk. "I might, depending on the conditions of course."

"Of course," Joanna said with another smile. "Very well, Ms Charbonneau. We'll talk again. Enjoy the rest of your evening." Joanna squeezed CC's shoulder lightly and added with a wink, "And don't believe rumors."

"I usually don't."

"Good. Remember they're rarely true." And with that she walked away and left CC alone with new hopes and a sense of pride in her work and in the company she worked for. CC looked down again to see if she could spot Liz. She saw Kayla instead, waving at her to get her attention with an alarmed look on her face. CC motioned for her to join her and Kayla quickly climbed the stairs.

When Kayla finally reached CC, she was completely out of breath. She leaned against the railing and breathed heavily, holding one finger in front of CC's face. "What the hell is going on, K?" CC asked impatiently.

"Okay. Listen, baby girl. I don't even know if I should tell you 'cuz I didn't see anything with my own eyes, but I can't keep what I've heard from you."

"What?"

"It's about Carrot-Bitch. Now like I said I don't know for sure it's true cuz I didn't see anything. But a few other girls did."

"What? What the hell? Just say it, K, you're driving me crazy." Kayla's hesitation made CC think it had to be something big. She felt her friend's hands grab her shoulders, and she watched her mouth move almost in slow motion as the words finally came out.

"Carrot-Bitch just gave Jeff Hudson a blow job right in the ladies' room."

CC collapsed against Kayla's body and screamed into her voluptuous breasts. "No!"

* * *

"There you are. I've been looking for you all over this boat," Liz said when she found CC standing alone outside on the first deck, close to the exit. CC wanted off this boat as soon as it would finally get back to the dock. She intended to wait there for Beth and hoped she would agree to give her a ride home.

She didn't want to confront Liz. But she couldn't act like everything was fine either. Her head was pounding. Joanna's and Kayla's words clashed against each other.

On one hand she wanted to listen to Joanna's words of wisdom and not believe rumors, but on the other hand she couldn't shake out of her mind the image of Liz on her knees in front of Jeff. Her guts told her this rumor was too appalling not to be true. Yet she had no proof. Kayla said some girls had seen it, but by the time the rumor got to Kayla "some girls" didn't even have names. She was certainly not going to ask Jeff Hudson, "Hey, Jeff, is it true my girlfriend just sucked you off?"

She started sobbing uncontrollably again. "CC, my love, what's going on?" Liz asked softly as she put her arms around CC and tried to turn her around so she could see her face.

"Get off me," CC said through clenched teeth as she violently shrugged off Liz's arms.

"CC, look at me. Please, tell me what's going on. I don't understand." Her voice was so sweet, so innocent, so loving.

"What's going on is I just heard about you and Jeff, Liz. So cut the act, will you?" CC was holding onto the rails so tightly her knuckles were white.

"Jeff? Jeff Hudson? Oh god. What did that asshole do to upset you now? Tell me, sweetie. I'll kick his ass." Again with that sweet, loving voice. Surely no one could be that deceitful, could they?

"Cut the crap, Liz. I know about the blow job! People saw you, for Christ's sake!"

CC had turned to face Liz when she spoke, and the surprise she saw on her face looked so genuine that Joanna's voice completely drowned out her own instincts. "Don't believe rumors." She saw Liz's expression turn from surprise to outrage and CC doubted herself even more.

"Who? Who, CC? Tell me who said they saw me...God I can't even say it. It's so disgusting. Tell me who said that, CC, please?"

"I don't know, I just heard it." CC wasn't going to name Kayla. She suddenly felt stupid for believing it so easily. She was going insane, she was convinced of it. Then Liz walked closer to CC and took her face, swollen with tears, in her soft hands. When Liz spoke, her voice was dainty and sounded so hurt.

"And you believed it? CC, don't you know how much I love you?" Tears fell down Liz's cheeks and CC decided she had to believe her. Liz was there, in front of her. She was real, unlike stupid rumors, and she loved her.

"It's not true?" she asked in a broken breath.

"Of course not, sweetie. Ask my friends. All I did all night was talk about you, how much I love you, and then look for you. I wanted to be with you, CC, dance with you. God, where were you all that time?"

"Looking for you," CC answered weakly before she let Liz wrap her arms around her and hold her tight. She cried again, this time with relief. Liz rubbed her back up and down in a calming motion until the tears subsided. Then she kissed her lips and leaned her forehead against CC's.

"My love, I'm so sorry someone told you these horrible things. I don't know why they wanted to hurt you so badly, but you have to believe me. I would never do anything to hurt you like that, CC. I love you. Please tell me you believe that."

"I do," CC breathed into Liz's mouth before kissing her. She pulled her close and watched over Liz's shoulder as their coworkers started gathering around them. CC hadn't realized the boat had finally made it to the dock. Beth was among the first in line to get off the boat. CC saw her and smiled. Beth smiled back very briefly but didn't hold CC's gaze. She walked past CC and Liz without looking their way again, and CC watched her back as she walked toward the parking lot.

CHAPTER TWELVE

CC was bent over in her living room tying up the laces of her running shoes when she felt Liz's hands on her buttocks. "Mm, look at that sexy ass," she growled behind CC. "Why don't you come back to bed, lover?"

CC straightened up and turned around to pull Liz into her arms. She placed a soft kiss on the adorable cleft of her chin before brushing her lips against those of the redhead, who quickly deepened the kiss while she let her hands roam over CC's body.

"Because I'll be late and I don't want to keep Beth waiting." Liz didn't even flinch at the drop of Beth's name. Instead she kept up her assault on CC's body, leaving a trail of open mouth kisses on her neck and collarbone. "Liz, I really have to go," CC murmured without much conviction.

Liz finally sighed with frustration and let her forehead drop to CC's shoulder. "Okay, woman. But just so you know, you're cruel."

"And you're insatiable, little minx."

"Yes, yes, I am. But it's all your fault. You keep getting more and more irresistible. I mean look at you." They giggled together, something they'd done a lot in the two weeks that had followed the dinner cruise in Lake George, and then CC pulled Liz into another tight embrace.

CC would never think of herself as irresistible, but the fifteen pounds she'd lost since she started running and the muscles she'd developed gave her more confidence in her own appearance than she'd ever experienced. She'd even purchased tighter active wear that showcased the natural curves of her body instead of covering them up. Today she was wearing dark grey shorts that hugged her hips and buttocks perfectly and a light blue T-shirt that clung to her shoulders, breasts and waist. Although she had to admit she did like the way she looked in her new clothes, she'd selected them because their aerodynamics made much more sense for a runner. Her baggy clothes had been getting in her way. She snickered at the thought. *A runner, really.*

"So, today's the day, huh?" Liz's voice forced CC out of her reverie.

"Yep, thirty minutes straight. All running." CC couldn't help the silly smile on her face.

"You can do it, poopsie. I'm so proud of you." Liz planted another kiss on CC's mouth.

CC was beginning the tenth and last week of her training program and was pleased with herself for reaching her goal. That, however, was only one reason why she felt so giddy. Her relationship with Liz had been so different since the dinner cruise, so much easier. There had been some outbursts on Liz's part, but they'd been less frequent, and CC sensed that they were well on their way to achieving the stability she craved.

Liz was headed back to school the following week, though. She hoped her new schedule would not interfere with their still fragile balance. She stuck out her bottom lip in what she hoped was an endearing little pout.

"I can't believe I won't get to see you at work every day anymore. I'll miss you."

"But you'll still see me every night. As long as you want me here."

"Every night it is then." CC kissed Liz tenderly before she broke their contact and started walking to the door. "All right, I really have to go. Will you be here when I get back?"

"No, I have some errands to run, and I have to drive to Saratoga to get some stuff from my parents' house. I'll drive straight to Manny's afterward. So I'll see you there?"

"Sounds good. See you then."

Liz's friends from Dixon & Brown had organized a small get-together to celebrate the end of Liz's brief career as a telemarketer and to wish her luck. Manny's was a tiny bar close to the office where D&B's employees often gathered for happy hour on Fridays. It would be CC's first time at Manny's in three years of employment, she mused as she ran down the stairs of her building. Strangely enough, the thought didn't provoke the same panic it had every time CC had considered going to happy hour back when she was still a phone rep and was still getting invited. She didn't particularly like the crowd that would be there, but they no longer intimidated her. She would face them and have the best time she could. For Liz's sake.

* * *

CC spotted Beth and Willow as soon as she parked her Jetta at the entrance of the park. They'd been running together three times a week for the past two weeks. CC enjoyed their runs immensely, and she would even admit that their recent partnership had helped keep her new passion for the sport alive and growing. As an experienced runner, Beth had a great number of tips to share, and she always seemed to find the right words to encourage CC every time she was ready to quit, which happened at least once or twice on every run.

"Hey," CC said to Beth as she patted Willow on the top of her large square head. She scratched the back of the dog's ears and smiled when Willow's tail started wagging energetically. "Hi Willow," CC started, taking a high-pitched, excited tone to address the animal. "Yeah, you're such a good girl. I'm happy to see you too, my good girl. Ready to run?" She brought her attention back to Beth when she heard the woman's familiar breathy chuckle. "What?"

"Nothing. I should be used to it. Willow gets all the attention and all I get is a 'hey.'" Beth shrugged and winked, clearly indicating she was joking.

CC would have normally laughed and dropped it. Since she was in a particularly giddy mood, however, her playful side came out before she could realize it. "What? You want me to scratch the back of your ears?" She raised her hand to the side of Beth's head and said in the same silly puppy talk she'd used with Willow, "You're a good girl too, Beth."

As soon as CC's fingers came in contact with Beth's thick dark blond hair, pulled back in a ponytail, Beth shivered and her eyes darkened. She covered CC's hand with her own and immobilized it against her cheek for a brief moment before bringing it back down to CC's side and releasing it. "That won't be necessary," she said in a barely audible voice. She smiled, but her eyes showed something else. Longing, perhaps, with a hint of pain.

"I'm sorry," CC said, feeling sincerely contrite down to her core although she wasn't sure why.

"Don't worry about it." Beth started walking with Willow, putting some distance between them, and her voice was back to its normal, even, friendly inflection when she continued, "Ready for your first *real* run?"

CC snorted a laugh and relaxed at Beth's tongue-in-cheek comment. "Hell yeah."

"Well, let's go then!" They walked for five minutes to warm up and then started running side by side, Willow between them. "Let me know if this is too fast."

"I'm good," CC said, feeling confident she could maintain their pace.

They ran in silence for ten minutes. That was the longest time CC had run without stopping until now: three intervals of ten minutes running and one minute walking. Proud of her new record, she kept on running with a grin on her mouth, thinking thirty minutes would be a piece of cake. Five minutes later, halfway through her run, all hell broke loose and she hit the proverbial wall. She could no longer get enough air into her lungs, sweat was burning her eyes and she was convinced her calves were going to split open.

"I need to walk for a minute," she managed to say between labored breaths.

"No," Beth replied firmly. She looked as fresh as ever, which infuriated CC. "We're going to slow down a bit, but we're not stopping, Ciel. We can push through this. It's temporary, I promise." Beth slowed down, and CC imitated her until their speed was barely faster than a walk. Yet they were definitely still jogging, not walking. "Don't forget to push all the air out of your lungs before you take another breath. There."

CC focused on her breathing, which she realized she'd forgotten all about for a minute.

"So, what do you have planned for the rest of the weekend?" CC rolled her eyes, knowing too well Beth was only trying to distract her. "Humor me, Ciel. You need to focus on something else, anything that's not the pain you're feeling now."

"I can't. It fucking hurts!" CC growled.

"No, it doesn't."

"Yes, it does."

"No. It does not, Ciel. Mind over body. Tell me about your weekend." CC understood she wasn't going to win the argument and decided to try it Beth's way.

"Housecleaning."

"Mhm," Beth simply prompted.

"Maybe a movie."

"Mhm."

"Going to Manny's tonight. Are you going?"

"No. You know I'm never invited to those things, Ciel."

"Would you come if I invited you?"

"Maybe. Think you can go faster now?"

CC realized the pain had faded considerably, and her breathing was still labored but controlled. "Yeah, let's go."

They increased their pace and maintained it until CC's watch beeped. Thirty minutes. Non-stop. They both breathed loudly and heavily. CC found the sound exhilarating. She felt no pain as they walked to cool down, their breathing slowly coming back to normal. She was on a high she'd never known before. A warm hand touched her back through the damp T-shirt.

"You did it." She looked at the woman who was staring at her with pride.

"Yeah, I did it. I fucking did it! Woohoo!" she yelled, not caring if anyone was around to hear her. "Thank you, Beth. For not letting me give up." She forced Beth to stop and face her so she could wrap her arms around the woman's waist and hug her. In a burst of energy her hug became so enthusiastic that she lifted Beth off the ground even though she was taller than CC. Beth gasped with surprise and started laughing as soon as her feet touched the ground again.

"You're crazy," she said as she wiped tears mixed with sweat at the corner of her eye. They started walking again. "I didn't do anything. Your legs, your run. It's all you, my dear."

"You know that's not true," CC said solemnly, her energy slowly coming down to a calmer level. "And about tonight, I'm officially inviting you, Beth. I would really like you to come. It'd be nice to have someone I can talk to."

Beth's gaze dropped down to her feet, showing her discomfort. "Oh, I don't know, Ciel. It'd make people uncomfortable. No one wants me there, believe me."

"I want you there," CC declared as she touched Beth's arm briefly. "Please? You know I hate these people."

Beth laughed and then smiled. She looked at CC straight in the eye, allowing CC to get lost in the bright green of her after-run eyes for a little while. CC was still looking for the right way to describe the color she'd never seen anywhere else. Beth hesitated a little longer, and CC could have sworn she regretted her next words as soon as they came out of her mouth. "Okay. I'll be there. What time?"

"Six."

* * *

It was a quarter after six when CC drove into Manny's parking lot. Alone in her apartment for the first time in several days, she'd taken an afternoon nap that lasted longer than she'd anticipated. Fortunately she'd already showered after her morning run, so as soon as she woke up she jumped into a pair of jeans and only hesitated a moment before she put on her new blouse, the daring black one that hugged her curves and exposed more cleavage than her usual clothes. She drove to Manny's as fast as she could within the limits of safety, mostly nervous about Beth. Beth was always on time. She would certainly resent CC for having to spend fifteen minutes alone with the wolves. CC got out of her Jetta and walked quickly toward the door.

"There you are," she heard behind her. She turned around and was instantly relieved when she saw Beth approach her. Beth's gaze dropped down to CC's blouse and CC saw her cheeks blush discretely. "Oh, you look stunning, Ciel."

CC felt her own cheeks heat up at the compliment before she replied, "Thank you. I'm so happy you just got here. I was afraid you'd be sitting in there in the middle of those people, hating my guts...Wait. You're late?"

"Well, not exactly," Beth admitted, embarrassed.

"You were waiting for me, weren't you?" CC wrinkled her nose and smiled at Beth to show she was teasing, "Needing my protection, Ms. Andrews?"

"Oh please, there was no way I was going to face that crowd without you. You're the one who invited me. There's really no point in being here if you're not." Beth swallowed, as if her last words had revealed too much. "I was waiting in my car."

"I get it," CC said, quickly rubbing Beth's shoulder to show her support and understanding. When her hand made contact with soft skin, CC was suddenly forced to take in Beth's attire, a sleeveless dark brown turtleneck and flattering tan chinos. "You look great, by the way."

"Thank you."

"All right, ready to face the voracious pack?"

"As ready as I'll ever be."

"Let's go." CC offered Beth one last comforting smile before she opened the door to the bar and entered slowly. The noise of the exuberant crowd and glasses and dishes clinking everywhere, the smell of fried food and stale air and the dark lighting immediately assaulted all of her senses. In dealing with Beth's nerves, she'd almost forgotten her own, but the stress suddenly came back rushing through her body with a vengeance. She turned to find Beth close behind her. It was the taller woman's turn to offer an encouraging smile, and they walked farther into the bar, looking for Liz and their coworkers.

Finally, still behind her, Beth extended one arm over CC's left shoulder and pointed to a table in the back of the bar, close to the restrooms. CC recognized most faces, but didn't see Liz. She froze until she finally spotted her gorgeous girlfriend coming out of the restroom. She smiled at the sight. Until she saw Jeff Hudson following the redhead back to the table and had to swallow around the lump that lodged in her throat. *What the fuck is he doing here?* She imagined her face was as white as the paper napkins sitting on every table when Liz, Jeff and their friends all turned to her and Liz motioned for her to join them with the most inviting smile on her full, freshly glossed lips.

"I can't stand this. Sorry." CC felt more than heard Beth say the words in her ear. When she turned to ask Beth what she meant, she was already out the door. CC held a finger up to communicate to Liz that she would be back in a minute before she followed Beth outside.

"Beth, wait. What's wrong? I know it's nerve-racking, but please don't leave me alone with them." She added a short laugh in an attempt to lighten the mood, but there was no humor in Beth's expression when she finally stopped walking toward her car and looked back to CC. She didn't appear nervous at all, but furious instead.

"I don't care about these people, Ciel. It's your girlfriend and that damn idiot Jeff Hudson that bother me. I can't sit in there..."

"I know," CC interrupted. "I didn't know Jeff would be here, and believe me I'm not happy about it at all, but that's only one more reason why I need you here with me for support."

"It's not just him, Ciel. Don't you see?"

"What do you mean?" CC's voice broke in the middle of her question and a ton of apprehension suddenly weighed on her heart. She watched as Beth walked closer and took her hands. Her rage had disappeared, replaced by concern, compassion, almost pity.

"I didn't want to tell you, Ciel. Maybe I should have, but it was really none of my business and I was afraid you'd think I was only telling you because…" Her voice trailed off. "Well anyway, I can't keep my mouth shut any longer, not while she keeps making a fool out of you."

CC remained silent, her eyes fixed on Beth's mouth, her hands squeezing Beth's. Recognition settled in. She knew what Beth was going to say. She didn't want to hear it but she couldn't move, unable to turn away from the train crash happening in front of her.

"I saw them that night on the boat, Ciel. Liz and Jeff. In the ladies' room."

CC's body doubled over and her breath was taken away as if she'd been punched in the stomach.

"I'm so sorry, Ciel," Beth murmured while she began rubbing CC's back.

CC suddenly straightened up and jerked Beth's hand away from her. "What Beth? What did you see exactly?" she asked through clenched teeth, surprised at her own contempt.

"I won't go into details, Ciel. That wouldn't be helpful."

"I need details, Beth!" CC was now shouting and Beth took a step back. "Tell me, was she on her knees in front of that asshole with his dick in her mouth? Did she enjoy it? Did she moan?" Sobs made it impossible for CC to continue her rampage. She looked at Beth, her eyes begging her to deny it all, to make her world right again.

Instead she saw Beth's eyes well up with tears before she nodded slowly. "I'm so sorry. So, so sorry," was all she said before tears started falling down her cheeks.

"CC, what the hell is taking you so long?"

CC looked over her shoulder to see Liz at the door. When she brought her gaze back to Beth, she was walking away.

"What the hell was she doing here? She wasn't invited."

"Shut up, Liz," CC said as she watched Beth get into her car.

"Seriously, CC, what were you thinking bringing her here? This is my party, after all. You had to know I wouldn't want her here."

"Shut up," CC repeated as Beth drove away.

"I mean she's so socially awkward. She doesn't know how to have fun. Good thing she's gone. Are you coming in or what? We're about to…"

"I said shut the fuck up, Liz!" She screamed the words at the top of her lungs. Yes, she was making a scene right outside of a bar, but she didn't care anymore. She spun around to face Liz so quickly she felt dizzy. "She saw you, Liz. Beth saw you and Jeff on the boat. Everything you denied and said you'd never have done because you love me so much, it was true all along."

"Oh god, not that again," Liz replied, rolling her eyes with exasperation. "Come on, CC. I thought we were over that. Are you really going to believe that woman over me?"

CC squared off her shoulders and stood straight before she declared without an ounce of hesitation, "Yes. That woman's never lied to me. I'll believe her over you any day, anytime. Now, tell me the fucking truth, Liz."

"Fuck you, CC Charbonneau. Why the hell would I say anything? Obviously whatever I say won't matter. You've already made up your mind!"

"I need to hear it from you, Liz. To know once and for all that I'm not crazy. Can you just do that one thing for me? Tell the fucking truth so I know I'm not going completely insane?"

CC saw Liz's face morph as she'd seen it so many times before, this time from a defiant air to a pitiful grimace as she prepared for her remorseful confession. CC didn't let Liz's instant tears affect her. She stood still and waited for the words she needed to hear.

"All right, all right, damn it, it's true. I'm so sorry CC."

She reached out to grab CC's hand, but CC stepped back, forcing Liz to lace her own fingers together in obvious embarrassment.

"I don't know why I did it. I do love you, CC. Oh God, I'm so fucked up."

Tears became sobs and soon Liz was crying so hard she seemed to have trouble breathing, snot mixing with tears. CC had no compassion left in her. All she saw was ugliness. All of Liz's ugliness finally exposed.

"Please, CC. Please, forgive me. You're the best thing that ever happened to me. Please, I know I fucked up. I can't lose you."

"Thanks for telling me the truth," CC said in a breath before she walked away. She never looked back, not even when Liz's pleas became louder, not even when she claimed she wanted to die.

* * *

"What is it, Mom?" CC asked her mother, standing breathless on the stoop of the small bungalow where she'd grown up. Instead of going home, CC had gone straight to her parents' house. She needed answers, to understand, and she was convinced her mother could help.

"Oh, honey, what on earth happened to you? Come in, sit down, and talk to me," Marie said as she guided CC to the tiny round table sitting in the middle of the kitchen. Charles briefly showed up but obediently went back to the living room when his wife waved him away. Obviously there was some kind of crisis, and Marie was the person to handle a crisis. He would come back for support once they were ready for him.

Once they were alone, Marie wrapped her hands around CC's tight fists on the table and met her distressed daughter's eyes with her own strong, calm, soothing deep blue stare. She held her gaze until CC's breathing became deeper and more regular.

"Tell me what's going on, honey. Whatever it is, I'll help you through it."

"It's Liz, Mom. What's wrong with her? I saw the way you looked at her when we had dinner a few weeks ago. Something's really wrong with her, mentally, and I think you know what it is. Please tell me."

Marie dropped her gaze to the table and sighed heavily. "Oh honey, I'm not a doctor. I can't diagnose…"

"Mom, stop it. I know you're not a doctor. But you've been working with mentally ill people for over thirty years. I'm not asking you for an official diagnosis. I'm asking you for your well-educated opinion. Please, I need to understand."

"Oh, my sweet baby, what did she do?"

"Mom, please. I need to know. I'll tell you everything, I promise."

"Okay, okay. From my experience, if I had to guess, I would say Liz suffers from something called Borderline Personality Disorder. You've probably heard me mention that disorder before. I've worked with several cases through the years."

CC sighed with relief, as if naming the problem had put it into a box that made it safer or at least more familiar and less threatening. "BPD, okay. Yes, that makes sense, I guess." CC didn't know much about the disorder, but she was still able to start slowly connecting some dots.

"Now will you please tell me what happened, honey?"

CC told her mother everything from the very beginning of her relationship with Liz, even Liz's confession regarding being molested. Every little detail seemed important, as if she wanted to provide her mother with every possible piece of the puzzle so they could understand it all together. CC thought her mother had probably never heard her, quiet CC, speak so many consecutive words.

CC used her finger to trace unrecognizable shapes on the wood of the table as she spoke, her eyes focused on her own hand while she searched for and recounted every event, every mood swing and every doubt she'd witnessed or experienced in the past nine weeks. She stopped to cry a few times, but Marie never interrupted until CC finished her narration and looked up to her mother.

"So what is it, Mom? What happened that night in my loft that made you see in one evening what I couldn't see in over two months? Was it just the mood swings?"

Marie took a hold of CC's hands again before she finally spoke. "Don't do that to yourself, honey. You couldn't know. Even with my experience I wasn't sure. I can't be sure even now. If I'd been sure, I would've said something, but I thought you were happy, really happy, so I put my suspicions aside. I'm sorry."

"Don't be. Honestly I probably wouldn't have been very receptive if you'd told me. I knew you saw something, but I wasn't ready to hear it. I figured, you know, she's an artist. She's emotional, that's all."

CC shrugged and smiled weakly at her mother as tears slowly escaped her already inflamed eyes once more. She took her hands from her mother's grip to quickly wipe her tears and sighed heavily before returning her hands to the table, this time reversing roles and holding her mother's hands instead of being held.

"So, now that you know everything, what do you think? Do you still think it's BPD? Or something else?"

Marie smiled before she spoke cautiously, "Everything I'm telling you is still nothing but my opinion, honey. It takes long weeks, sometimes even years and a team of professionals to properly diagnose a mental illness and even then mistakes are made. That said, the more you tell me about Liz the more I think it's BPD. Everything is there. The mood swings, the insecurities, the fear of abandonment, the self-deprecation.

"But that's not all. You know, Liz has probably always been extremely emotional, impulsive and sensitive, even as a child. And you're right: those are traits we often associate with artists because somehow many of them seem to feel so much more than the rest of us, which allows them to create the beautiful art they give us. Not all artists are like that, that's for sure, but I can imagine Liz could have grown up to be a highly emotional yet well-balanced artist. Having strong emotions doesn't mean you'll suffer from BPD, honey."

CC squinted at her mother, grasping to every word. "It doesn't?" she asked, impatient to hear the rest of her mother's explanation and at the same time wondering why it was so important for her to understand Liz. Why she couldn't simply categorize her as a cheater and move on.

"No. It takes a lot more than that. A tendency to extreme, impulsive emotions is only one part of it. The dangerous part comes when those feelings and emotions are not validated in the environment in which children like Liz grow up. From what you told me it seems obvious Liz's parents have never accepted or even acknowledged the fact that being an artist could be an option for her. I can only imagine this was not the only desire or feeling of Liz's that they attempted or even succeeded to kill. That kind of invalidating behavior from her parents over time would be enough for a child like Liz to develop Borderline Personality Disorder, but…"

Marie stopped talking and closed her eyes before she sighed deeply.

"But what, Mom?"

"I already said too much, honey. I really can't know for sure anything I'm telling you is true."

"But you have a feeling about something else, don't you?" Marie nodded. "Please tell me, Mom. I don't understand why, but this, talking to you, it's helping me for some reason. I want to know what you're thinking."

"Okay, honey, if it can help. But remember it's nothing more than my opinion."

"I know. Please continue."

"Well, you told me her grandfather molested her. Did she tell you if she told her parents about it?"

CC thought back to that emotionally draining night and regretted not asking questions. "No, all she said was that she didn't see her grandfather again and he died not too long afterward."

"Okay. I can't know for sure, but my instinct tells me that little five-year-old Liz probably did tell her parents about it. And they probably didn't believe her or told her she exaggerated and quickly swept the incident under the rug."

CC's heart dropped to her stomach and her mouth became dry. She took a sip of water and looked at her mother with a mix of incredulity, fear and disgust. "What? But how? How could parents ignore that sort of thing? Does that really happen?"

"More often than you want to know, honey. Especially when the molestation is done by a family member. As you can imagine, that would be one of the worst ways to invalidate a child."

"The worst. Oh my god." Chills crept up CC's skin, leaving her arms with goose bumps. She wanted to cry again, for Liz, but her eyes only burned and her throat was too tight to breathe, let alone cry. She and her mother stared at each other silently. Marie's eyes spoke of the horrors she'd heard in her long career and CC's answered with the endless compassion she felt rising within her. It took several minutes before she was finally able to speak.

"So what do I do now? Abandon her? Support her and forget my own feelings? She did cheat on me, Mom." She looked to her mother, desperate for an answer, for guidance.

"Oh god, honey, that's a very difficult question. If Liz were being treated and if I were her case manager I'd tell her to hold on to you with everything she's got. You're the perfect partner for someone suffering with BPD. You're patient, compassionate, understanding…" Marie's voice trailed off and she gazed at CC with pride before she lowered her eyes to their joined hands and cleared her throat to continue, "But Liz is not in treatment. She hasn't even been diagnosed yet. And as your mother, my sweet, sweet girl, I have to tell you to run like hell. Run away and don't look back. She doesn't mean to, but she's not done hurting you, honey, not by a long shot."

CC nodded sadly. She stayed with her mother for another hour. Marie handed her one of her friends' business cards. A therapist. She suggested it would be a good idea for CC to talk to someone who wasn't a family member. CC took the card and slipped it into her back pocket without looking at the name. She didn't think she could go through this story again. Eventually

Charles joined them and they shared a glass of wine. Not much was said, but they sat together and CC let their presence cradle her. When she left, she had not yet decided what she would do, but she knew without a shadow of a doubt that she had never felt so grateful for being raised by this particular couple of hippy-wannabes.

* * *

It was past ten p.m. when CC entered her loft. All she wanted was to climb in bed and sleep. Her brain and her body were exhausted. She needed to turn off the lights on everything that had happened and revisit it in the morning.

As soon as she saw Liz's sexy stilettos by the door she understood that would not be possible. She felt nauseous. She hadn't made any decision yet regarding their relationship, but she knew the night's events and especially her conversation with her mother had left her too vulnerable to face Liz now. She wasn't ready.

"I'll have to get that key back," she said out loud. It was only then that she realized there was no one around to hear her. She found it perplexing. If Liz was here, why was the loft so overwhelmingly quiet?

She took off her own shoes by the door and walked slowly to the bedroom, imagining and hoping that Liz would be in bed, sleeping. CC would grab her pillow and an extra blanket from her closet and crash on the couch. They could talk tomorrow. Maybe CC would know what she wanted to do in the morning and would be better prepared for their inevitable conversation.

In the darkness of the bedroom she saw that the bed appeared untouched and no human shape seemed to hide under the covers. She turned on the light to make sure. The sudden brightness made her squint, but she was able to confirm the bed was empty. *What the hell.*

CC walked back to the living space of the loft and turned on every light. Liz wasn't sleeping on the couch, not smoking by the open window, not making a cup of coffee in the kitchen.

Walking toward the bathroom, she saw that the door was ajar and light was peeking through. Her guts immediately twisted. Something was wrong. She increased her pace and knocked lightly on the door.

"Liz, are you okay?" She waited for Liz's answer for only a second and when none came she pushed the door open.

She didn't recognize her own voice when a scream from deep inside her emptied her lungs. She gasped for air, frozen at the door, staring at the scene in front of her. All she saw was blood. Blood all over Liz's arms and on the white tiles of the floor.

Finally, under all the blood, she saw Liz. She was sitting on the floor between the sink and the toilet, leaning her back against the wall, her arms and hands resting on her bent knees, palms up. It was clear the blood had come from cuts on her arms. Several cuts. CC didn't know how many there were, but most of Liz's pale skin was covered with blood.

"Liz? Liz can you hear me?" CC knew the words came from her own mouth, but her voice was so weak it seemed to originate from very far away. Liz was conscious but unresponsive. She was staring blankly at the wall in front of her and taking quick, shallow breaths through her mouth. Her face was pale, her eyes swollen with recent tears, her red hair sticking to her perspiring forehead and her neck. She was wearing nothing but a black bra and matching panties.

CC looked at the blood dripping from Liz's arm down to the floor and saw a small razor blade at Liz's feet, still stained with Liz's blood. The sight of the cold object forced her back to reality. Liz had hurt herself and she had to react.

"Liz," she said louder in a more commanding voice. Liz kept staring at the wall. CC ran to the living room to get to the phone. She dialed 911 and took the phone back with her to the bathroom where she described the scene to the dispatcher. Soon she was assured an ambulance was on the way and she kept talking, every sentence ending with "so much blood."

CHAPTER THIRTEEN

CC got out of bed. She couldn't sleep. Back at her loft since the early hours of the morning, she'd been unable to shut down her brain. She'd left the hospital after she was certain Liz was going to be okay. She'd scrubbed the bathroom floor until she could no longer see a speck of blood and then, feeling tired, gone to bed. It was now eleven in the morning and she hadn't gotten a minute of sleep. She was too restless. She officially gave up and got dressed in running clothes, her mind racing.

She felt guilty for leaving the hospital, but Liz wasn't alone. Her parents were with her. Liz had been given a heavy dose of sedatives in the ambulance on their way to the hospital. Before she fell asleep she had just enough time to ask CC to call her parents.

CC cringed, her disdain for Mr. and Mrs. McLeary still much too raw, but she called them anyway. Liz still needed them, no matter how they might have raised or damaged her.

CC had stayed with Liz until they arrived. While she waited the doctor told her that although the scene she'd witnessed must have been very scary, the multiple cuts Liz had inflicted on herself were superficial. None was deep enough to cause severe injuries and none would leave a permanent scar. What remained unsaid was that the real thing to be concerned about was Liz's state of mind.

When Liz's parents arrived, the doctor asked to meet with them to discuss the next steps. CC was clearly not invited to partake in the discussion. The couple didn't even acknowledge her presence. She left, hoping this would be the wake-up call Liz's parents needed to see how much their daughter needed help. It sure had been a wake-up call for her.

She wanted to talk to her mother about the incident, but not now. Now she needed to run. She was so tense she wanted to crawl out of her own skin. She needed to channel all that negative energy into an activity that would leave her body drained and her mind empty.

Another need showed up unannounced when she finished tying up her shoes, grabbed her cell phone and prepared to leave. It wouldn't be denied. She dialed Beth's phone number. CC sighed when the soothing voice answered and then asked, "Hey there, are you up for a run?"

* * *

CC met Beth and Willow at the park and recounted the events of the night while they walked briskly to warm up. Beth listened with empathy despite her antipathy toward Liz.

"That's terrible, Ciel. I'm so sorry. I don't really know what to say, but I'm sure the hospital is the best place for Liz right now. They'll be able to help her."

"I know." CC's tone was defensive. She'd told Beth about her long night without feeling or showing any sadness, anger or fear, as if simply enumerating facts. Beth's compassion now irritated her.

After a long uncomfortable silence, Beth dared talking again. "I'm glad you called. I thought you'd be angry with me."

"Why would I be angry with you?" CC noted how flat her own voice sounded.

"I'm not sure. For not telling you about what I saw earlier. Or for telling you last night. Maybe for both."

"Oh." More unwelcome questions CC would need to examine soon. She regretted calling Beth. She didn't need to add more debates to her already jumbled mind. Then one question popped up and came out of her mouth before she realized it.

"Why tell Kayla? If you didn't want to tell me that night, why did you tell Kayla?"

"What?" Beth's expression was one of sheer confusion.

"Kayla's the one who told me that night about the rumor."

"I assure you, Ciel. Kayla didn't hear it from me. No one did. I never told a soul about what I saw that night until I told you. I'm sure other women saw them though. They weren't exactly discrete, you know."

"Yeah right." *Enough. Enough talking.* CC couldn't think one more second. She started running without warning Beth and she was at least ten feet in front of the other woman and her dog before they started running to catch up with her. Setting a pace that was faster than usual, she soon was forced to focus on her breathing so she could push forward.

She forgot about Beth's and Willow's presence; she was running alone. Slowly other thoughts were replaced with the sound of her breathing and her running shoes hitting the gravel of the path under her feet. She welcomed the pain in her calves, her shins and her thighs. She enjoyed the burning sensation of salty sweat on her face. The sun was strong, her lungs kept air flowing in and out, albeit with gradually increasing difficulty. She forgot about time; her watch had stayed home. She just ran and kept running until a firm voice finally reached her.

"Stop! That's enough! You're going to hurt yourself!"

CC recognized the voice as Beth's although it came from several feet behind her. She slowed down and immediately felt dizzy, as if a spell had been broken. She spotted a trash can next to a bench on the side of the path and barely reached it before she started retching. Nothing but bile came out, reminding her that she hadn't fed herself since the previous afternoon. It hurt like hell. She felt Beth's hand on her back, moving in circular motions while she spoke with concern.

"Oh my god, Ciel. I shouldn't have let you run like that. You had no sleep, and probably no food in I don't know how long. I'm so sorry."

CC muttered something Beth couldn't understand.

"What?"

CC let herself fall on her back in the grass next to the trash can and repeated between labored breaths, "You couldn't have stopped me."

"I could've tried." Beth sat down in the grass and placed a hand on CC's clammy forehead. She delicately smoothed wet strands of hair off the damp skin. Meanwhile Willow lay down next to CC and rested her large Boxer head on her thigh. Beth's voice was almost a whisper but it couldn't cover a hint of panic, "Talk to me, Ciel. Are you feeling all right? Do you want me to drive you to the hospital?"

"No. No, I'll be okay," CC answered in a breath. She took the hand that was still on her forehead and brought it to her stomach.

Beth understood the silent request and flattened her palm against CC's diaphragm. "There you go. In…and out," she said softly as CC breathed, pushing against Beth's hand when she inhaled and then letting the heaviness of Beth's hand help her get all the air out of her lungs when she exhaled. Her breathing finally slowing down, CC relaxed and became more conscious of the weight of Willow's head on her thigh and Beth's touch on her stomach. She allowed their comforting presence to soothe her. Soon, however, her stomach began contracting again and the sobbing she'd held inside since she'd found Liz bleeding on her bathroom floor finally came to the surface, powerful, loud and uncontrollable. She turned into Beth's lap and wrapped her arms around her waist, bawling the entire night out of her body.

"Oh, my poor Ciel. That's right, cry it all out. I'm here," Beth said in a low and tender voice that, paired with strong hands rubbing her back, made CC feel completely safe.

* * *

After her run and the cathartic crying fit that followed it, CC went back to her loft, showered, ate a peanut butter sandwich and took a nap. She felt human again when Liz called around dinner time and asked her to come to the hospital. The invitation terrified CC and she wanted to refuse. She didn't think she could face another emotion-filled evening. Liz sensed her hesitation and insisted that her visit was very important to her. When she was assured that they would be alone, CC finally conceded. Deep down she did want to see how Liz was doing and what steps had been taken to help the young woman. The young woman she still loved, despite everything.

When she entered the hospital, however, panic settled in again. Her heart pounded as she tentatively made her way to Liz's room. Then she saw the weak smile on the face she worshiped and couldn't help smiling back. Liz looked so young in her hospital bed. Free of makeup and wearing a thin hospital gown, she exuded nothing of her usual irresistible sexiness. CC was relieved to see her so vulnerable, especially since her own heart was still raw with pain, fear and confusion.

"Hey," CC said as she entered the room, looking around to make sure they were alone.

"They went to dinner. I asked them to give me an hour with you," Liz offered to further reassure CC. Her voice was so timid it made her sound like a little girl. "Would you please have a seat?"

"Sure." CC sat on the lone uncomfortable plastic chair by Liz's bed and rubbed her hands nervously on her jean-clad thighs. She noticed only a little of Liz's arms were still bandaged and the cuts that had been so scary less than twenty-four hours ago looked like tiny scratches. She guessed the few smaller bandages that remained covered the worst of the cuts. She examined the exposed scratches and suddenly remembered seeing similar ones on Liz's arms before, although certainly not that many. Liz had told CC her roommate's cat had scratched her and CC hadn't seen any reason not to believe her. She sighed, wondering how many more lies and cover-ups would reveal themselves in the coming days or weeks. She hated the fact that she was being forced to question their entire relationship. "How are you feeling?" she finally asked with genuine interest.

"Better," Liz said, looking at the cuts on her arms. She smiled and brought a finger to her own temple before she continued, "But in there I'm still a mess and the doctors tell me it'll be a while before we know what the problem is and how to treat it." Her green eyes briefly sparkled with tears, but she blinked them away. "That's why I wanted to see you tonight. I'm transferring to Four Winds tomorrow, and I didn't want to go without seeing you."

"Four Winds as in the psychiatric hospital in Saratoga?"

"Exactly," Liz admitted with a chuckle, embarrassed. "I'll go through a bunch of tests and hopefully they'll help me find out what's wrong with me and come up with a plan for me to get better."

Tears flowed to Liz's cheeks this time, and CC was compelled to reach out and wipe them with her thumb. Liz pushed her cheek against CC's palm and their eyes met. CC couldn't help but feel like she was meeting Liz for the first time.

When Liz pressed her lips against CC's hand, the tenderness was too overwhelming for CC to endure. She took her hand back and sat straight in the small chair. She cleared her throat. "That's good, Liz. I'm sure they'll be able to help you. Do you have any idea how long you'll be gone?" CC was torn between sadness at the thought of Liz leaving and relief that there would be more distance between them.

"No one knows. I'm dropping out of my classes for this semester. Then we'll see."

CC swallowed hard. "Okay. And was that the doctor's idea? Or your parents'?"

"Both, but in the end we all agreed. I want to get better, CC. I really do." The last words, barely a whisper, caught in Liz's throat as her voice broke.

"Good. That's all that matters." CC reached out to Liz again, this time to hold her hand.

Liz squeezed CC's hand and took a deep breath before she spoke again with both strength and resignation, in her attitude as much as in her voice. "It will be perfect. My parents' house is very close to the hospital and they promised they would be with me every step of the way. They've been very supportive, CC, more so than ever before."

CC smiled. "I'm very happy to hear that. You have no idea."

"So anyway, I wanted to see you before I go because, well, first I wanted to thank you for taking me to the hospital and taking care of me the way you did. The nurses told me you stayed here with me until my parents arrived. I hurt you terribly, CC, and you could've just put me in the ambulance and washed your hands of me. God knows I would've understood if you had."

"I could never do that, Liz. I don't understand everything that happened or why you cut yourself but I couldn't wash my hands of you, as you say."

"I know. You're too good of a person, CC. And just so you know, I don't understand everything either. I don't understand anything at all, actually. That's why I'm going to Four Winds. As far as the cutting goes, weirdly enough it made me feel better. It relieved me from the intense guilt and all the emotions I was dealing with last night. Even if it was just temporary relief. I don't expect you to get it. I know it sounds crazy."

CC only had to bring herself back to her morning run, when the physical pain had helped her through her own feelings, to understand at least partially what Liz was saying. "I see," she simply offered.

"The second reason I wanted to see you was to tell you again how terribly sorry I am for what I did with Jeff. I really have no explanation for it, but I promise that as soon as I do I'll let you know, if you want to hear it."

CC rubbed the back of Liz's hand with her thumb. "I'll want to hear it, yes. Whenever you find out."

Liz smiled and seemed encouraged to continue. "Last but not least, I wanted to ask you if there was any way you'd consider waiting for me. I know I have no right to ask you this, CC, but I'd never forgive myself if I didn't at least try. Even with everything that happened and all the questions I have, there's one thing that's still clear to me and that I hope you can find in your heart to believe, and that's that I do love you, CC. I love you with all of my fucked-up being and the fact that I messed up what I had with you is what hurts me the most in all of this. I want to get better for myself, but I also want to get better so I can be a woman who deserves your love, CC."

Liz had spoken so fast she was out of breath. She started crying again, this time harder, and CC stood up so she could hold her. As Liz sobbed against her chest, she carefully thought of how she would answer.

Funnily enough she did believe Liz loved her. She wasn't sure if it was because of the moments they'd shared or because she simply needed to believe that it was true, that she couldn't have been that much of a fool, but she did believe Liz's love for her was genuine. She would even go as far as stating that Liz loved her as much and as well as she was capable of given her circumstances.

As sure as she was of Liz's love, however, a new certitude was slowly taking root. Her mother's words played over and over again in her mind: "Run like hell." She could not, would not support Liz through her illness as a partner or a lover. It was a matter of self-preservation. She held Liz tighter against her chest and spoke with resolve. "I will be here for you through all of this, Liz, but only as a friend. That's the best I can do." She let Liz cling to her when she started crying even harder.

CHAPTER FOURTEEN

Kayla took one last hit of her blunt and let the fire go out before putting the cigar away in the small tin box she always carried in her purse. She still tried to hand the blunt to CC once in a while, proving that old habits did indeed die hard, but not this morning. CC was pensive and quiet on their drive to work, and Kayla seemed deeply annoyed. "You didn't hear a word I said, did you?"

CC looked at her friend with a sheepish grin. "No, sorry K. I pretty much lost you at 'you won't believe what my asshole of a boyfriend did this time.'"

"That's what I said when I first got in the car, CC. Wow. I've been talking to myself for ten fucking minutes."

"I know, I'm sorry. I have a lot on my mind. Go ahead, I'm listening now." She took her eyes off the road long enough to make eye contact with Kayla and let her know she had her undivided attention. Kayla's eyes were nothing but slits, and she started snickering as CC brought her attention back to the road.

"Oh hell, CC. I can't remember now." She waved a dismissive hand in front of her face. "Don't worry about it. I bet Damon won't listen any more than you did when I start telling him what an asshole my friend CC is." They both laughed. "So what's on your mind anyway? Did you get another email from Lezzie McCrazy?"

CC lightly slapped Kayla's thigh. "I told you not to call her that, K. She's not crazy. She's sick."

"Oh, leave me alone with your PC bullshit. Did she email you again, yes or no?"

"Yes."

It was the second email she received from Liz in the four weeks since she'd seen her in the hospital before she left for Saratoga. One month. CC still cried herself to sleep every night. Sometimes she cried over the loss of a relationship, like anyone suffering from a broken heart would. Those nights were strangely comforting. They made sense. Other times she cried over the alarming thought that the only woman who'd ever been able to light up every fiber of her being was so severely mentally ill. She hated those nights. They left her hopeless and doubting her own sanity. She still had the card her mother had given her and she often considered making an appointment with Dr. Simmons, but she hadn't yet, not convinced her own problems warranted the help of a professional.

Liz's first email had come after two weeks of silence. It was more like a progress report than anything else. Liz explained that she was out of the hospital and staying with her parents. Her doctors had officially diagnosed her with Borderline Personality Disorder. She was prescribed medication and the long-term plan was for her to see a psychiatrist as an outpatient to continue her dialectical behavior therapy. CC's mother had confirmed dialectical behavior therapy was common for BPD patients. It was designed to give them the skills they needed to better understand their emotions, deal with crisis and distress and eventually maintain good relationships. It sounded a lot more complex than that, of course, but that was how CC understood it.

That first email had put a smile on CC's face. She was still upset, but knowing Liz was getting the help she needed consoled her to a certain extent. At least something was going in the right direction. The second email, the one she'd received last night, was different.

"So?" Kayla asked impatiently.

"So what?"

"What the fuck did the email say? Damn, baby girl, stay with me for half a second, will you? It's like pulling teeth."

"Well, she's still in therapy. Learning a lot about herself and all that good stuff."

"And?"

"And what?"

"Come on, CC. I know there's more."

CC hesitated before she talked about the part of the email that had her in turmoil. "Okay, okay. She said she misses me. She still loves me and hopes I can give her another chance when she feels better."

Kayla sighed deeply. "You told her to go fuck herself right?"

"No," CC admitted. "I didn't answer yet." She held on to the steering wheel tightly and finally spoke the whole truth. "She got to me, K. I do miss her so much."

"Oh no, no you fucking don't." Kayla's tone was firm and agitated. "Don't you fucking dare let that bitch get to you. What the fuck is wrong with you? I wish you'd get angry already."

"You know I can't be angry with her. She's sick, K. And how would that help anyway?"

"Oh, shut the fuck up with the sick crap already! Sick or not, the bitch lied to you, she drove you crazy and she cheated on you. She *did* do all of that shit, CC! She did it to you and you're allowed to be pissed off about it. You *need* to be pissed off about it. Anger is an important part of healing, you know that. All your understanding bullshit is not helping you and it's driving me mad. Please, CC, just tell me you'll stay strong. You can't let her get to you."

"I won't. I promise, K. Thank you." She squeezed her friend's hand in gratitude as they pulled into the D&B parking lot. CC knew she'd needed Kayla's honest kick-in-the-ass speech. Ultimately she'd decided to tell her friend about Liz's email knowing she would go off and tell her exactly what she needed to hear.

No, she couldn't let Liz get to her. She couldn't go back to that relationship, even if Liz did get better, which would take a lot longer than a month. CC even knew Kayla was right about anger. It was a necessary step to her recovery. She knew it was in her, somewhere, but every time it tried to flair up it was smothered with compassion. CC wanted to hate Liz, she really did, but when she attempted to hate the woman she saw the child that was molested and then denied so much as the acknowledgment from her own parents that the molestation had happened in the first place. She shook the thought away and followed Kayla into the building.

* * *

"Today is the day," Beth said excitedly as she leaned against CC's desk. CC looked up at the taller woman, and although Beth's words puzzled her she couldn't help but smile at the mischievous sparkle in the green eyes. Then again, smiling came naturally when she was in Beth's presence.

Although she was still crying every night, CC's days were good for the most part, sprinkled at times with moments of true happiness. That was thanks to Beth and their growing friendship. They ran together three times a week, ate lunch together Monday through Friday (more often than not leftovers Beth had cooked the night before) and shared conversations that were smart, stimulating and wonderfully distracting. CC found spending time with Beth easy and reassuring. She knew Beth enjoyed it just as much. She smiled more often and Kayla had even mentioned that some of their coworkers had caught a glimpse or two of the happier, warmer version of Beth that CC was familiar with. In fact, the glacial Beth everyone was used to was making herself scarce these days.

Even her appearance had changed. CC suspected she might be the only one noticing that more subtle transformation; she wasn't entirely certain it wasn't her own perception that had changed. Either way she saw Beth in a different light, or perhaps she simply saw her at last.

Today for example, Beth wore the same type of button-down business shirt she wore most work days. It was professional, classic and so Beth. CC couldn't decide, however, if the brick-red shirt had a tighter fit than others, if one more button was left open or if she simply allowed herself to notice for the first time that Beth had breasts. Probably two full C-cups worth of beautiful, round breasts.

She couldn't explain the sudden realization. For most of the two years she'd worked closely with Beth, she'd never really looked at her. She'd barely noticed Beth was a woman, let alone that she could be attractive, and now, only one month after a still painful breakup, while her mind was still full of Liz, here she was, staring at Beth's breasts. She blinked and shook her head. When she opened her eyes again, she made sure they stayed focused on Beth's eyes and nothing lower.

"What day is that?" she asked.

"Joanna's going to do it today. He's finally out, Ciel." Beth brought a hand to her neck and slid her finger from one side to the other, imitating the movement of a knife slitting a throat to illustrate her point.

"You're kidding me."

"I kid you not, my friend. We will be rid of asshole Jeff Hudson by the end of the day."

"Oh my god, at last."

"At last, indeed."

Their entire conversation was whispered so no one, especially not Kayla, could hear. Joanna had trusted Beth and CC with her plans because she needed their help to gather enough dirt on Jeff to justify firing him, but she'd made them promise to remain discrete. Discretion, of course, wasn't a problem for Beth and CC. Since Joanna and CC had talked during the dinner-cruise, CC had been sending daily reports of every single lead she disqualified as well as the reasons why it was disqualified directly to Joanna on top of sending the same reports to Jeff as usual. It had been easy for Joanna to compare those daily reports with those that Jeff sent his clients and see that nearly ninety percent of disqualified leads ended up being sent to clients despite CC's recommendations. This lack of regard for quality was only one part of the puzzle. Beth and CC knew Joanna had worked several other angles to gather proof of Jeff's incompetence, and they'd been growing impatient for the day he would finally get fired.

"Why today? Did something happen?

"Our biggest client called Joanna yesterday to complain about him. That put the final nail in his coffin. Oh, how I would love to be a fly on the wall when Joanna tears him a new asshole." CC burst out laughing, which made Beth giggle lightly before she asked, "What, why are you laughing?"

"Sorry. I'm still not used to hearing you talk that way. You've always been so proper."

Beth smiled and stared at CC through eyelashes that had never looked so long. "I thought you were getting to know me better than that, Ciel."

"I am. But you still surprise me."

"Oh, I see. Well, that can be a good thing right?"

The tone of the conversation had definitely shifted, and CC wasn't certain what was happening. Beth was still whispering, but her throaty voice suddenly seemed to lean more on the sexy side.

"Very good," CC conceded.

Beth closed her eyes, and when she reopened them they were filled with sadness. "I will miss you," she said in a breath.

CC had told Beth all about Joanna's inquiry regarding her potential interest in a position as client relationship manager, a position that would be vacant as soon as Jeff was shown the door. Beth encouraged CC, assuring her she would be a great fit for the job. CC knew she couldn't refuse the opportunity for advancement and was confident she could do very well in such a position. They both knew it was the right thing for CC to do, but what had remained unsaid was that they would each miss the working relationship and the connection they'd developed in the past two years. CC loved QA, and she loved working with

Beth even more. Now CC's impending departure from the QA department was very real and what had been left unsaid needed to be heard.

"QA won't be the same without you, Ciel," Beth added before her voice broke.

"I will miss you too." Before she realized what she was doing, CC rolled her chair to face Beth, who was still leaning against her desk. She placed both of her hands on Beth's thighs and rubbed them to comfort her as she looked up to hold her gaze. "But we'll still see each other every day. We can still have lunch together, and we'll keep running. Everything doesn't need to change, Beth."

CC grinned with satisfaction when her words managed to force a timid smile on Beth's mouth.

"It doesn't. You're right. Actually," Beth stopped talking and bit her lower lip, something CC knew she did when she started to express a thought but then regretted it and didn't want to finish. For some reason CC really wanted to hear this particular thought.

"Actually what, Beth?"

"Well, I was thinking maybe," she hesitated again and closed her eyes before she continued, "Maybe we could do other stuff together outside of work, besides running I mean. Maybe I could cook for us this Friday and we could watch a movie or maybe some *Buffy*? Just a thought."

CC's grin extended from ear to ear, which immediately reassured Beth and allowed her to smile back. "Your cooking and some *Buffy*? How can I say no to that?" CC wondered if she sounded flirtatious and then realized she was still rubbing Beth's thighs, albeit more slowly, perhaps even sensuously. She lingered a few more seconds, allowing her hands to feel the runner's strong muscles, before she quickly brought her hands to her own lap. "I really enjoy our friendship. Beth. I'll only be too happy to spend more time with you. You can definitely count on me for Friday." She consciously stopped short of adding "It's a date." She did not want Beth to think it was a date. It was definitely not a date.

"Great, I'll be looking forward to it. Is chili okay?"

"You know I love your chili."

"All right then. Chili it is." Beth winked at her before she left her cubicle and for the first time in weeks CC started actively looking forward to the weekend.

* * *

CC sat on her couch with her laptop, staring at the screen. She'd read Liz' email at least a hundred times. The beginning of the message was nice. Liz enjoyed therapy and was slowly learning new skills and understanding herself better. She admitted there was a lot more work to be done, but she was hopeful. The last paragraph was the one CC couldn't help going back to over and over again.

I miss you so much, CC. I miss being held by you every night and waking up with you every morning. I miss our silliness while cooking together or watching TV. I miss staring at your ass in those ridiculously sexy shorts you wear to run. I miss our dirty talk, the way you tremble under my touch and the way you moan just before you come. I can't stop thinking about our life together, CC, and I can't help hoping you can forgive me. The irrational hope that I might get to love you and be loved by you again some day is what keeps me going. I know it's much too soon, but I needed you to know. I still want you, my sweet CC. I will never give up.

All my love,

Your Liz

CC realized she was caressing the keyboard of her laptop with her fingertips and her mouth was dry. She'd already typed up three potential replies but had deleted all of them.

The first one had been easy, because it said what her heart really wanted to say. "I miss you too. Please get better and come back to me. I love you." It was the answer she couldn't afford, the one that would leave her vulnerable, the one that would make her suffer even more. Not to mention Kayla would kill her. And she would deserve it. She knew that. Going back to Liz would be plain stupid.

In her second reply, CC had admitted that she missed Liz and still loved her but said that she didn't think getting back together would be a good idea. It left all kinds of doors open, which was pretty much as bad as the first option. She was tempted to send it anyway, probably because deep down she wanted Liz to keep fighting for them, to keep trying to convince her it was actually a good idea. Which was also plain stupid.

In her third attempt CC had been firm, stating they would never get back together and Liz should give up on that hope. She read her own words several times and thought Kayla would be proud. She let the cursor hover over the "send" button for a long time but decided once again not to send it. She deleted it and quickly typed up a fourth one.

Hi Liz,

I'm so glad your therapy is going well and you're making progress. Things are going well for me too. I think I will be promoted soon, which is exciting. I'll give you more details when it's official. I have to run for now but please keep me posted. I like knowing how you're doing.

Take care,

CC

She hit the "send" button and quickly closed her laptop before she sighed with frustration. "When in doubt, avoid," she muttered to herself.

* * *

After work on Friday CC went home to shower and change before going to Beth's for dinner as planned. She'd recently purchased new clothes for the fall, but September had been too warm to wear any of them. Tonight promised to be chilly so she would finally get a chance to wear something new. Something Beth had not seen yet. The thought made her smile.

Fall was CC's favorite season, especially when it came to clothes. She loved the feeling of warmer, cozy sweaters. In the past she'd also enjoyed warmer clothes because they made it easier to cover her excess weight. This season, however, she'd discovered that there was such a thing as a cozy yet sexy sweater. She'd purchased a few of them, and tonight she chose a dark grey boat-neck knit; she loved the way her breasts looked in it. There was no harm in admitting it, was there? She wore the sweater with her favorite new blue jeans, the ones that were made to look faded in all the right places and had a tiny, strategically placed rip on one thigh. The look was casual but gave her the kind of confidence only new clothes could. She even wore some makeup for the occasion. It wasn't a date but that didn't mean it wasn't worth a minimal effort.

CC had never been to Beth's house before. She knew it was close to work and the park where they ran, but Beth had offered no description beyond the address and the color of the house. She smiled when she parked her Jetta behind Beth's car in a long and narrow driveway in front of a charming, tiny bungalow. It was covered in light grey siding with white trim and the window shutters were painted the same deep red as the front door. CC knew there hadn't been new construction in this neighborhood since the early eighties so Beth's home had to be at least thirty years old, but she obviously took very good care of it and its meticulous landscaping. She didn't expect anything less from Beth. She grabbed the bottle of wine she'd brought and made her way down a cobblestone path to the front door where she smiled again at the absence of a doorbell before using the classic aged iron door knocker to announce her arrival.

When Beth opened the door, CC had to keep her jaw from dropping. She wore a faded pink off-the-shoulder T-shirt with blue jeans that fit her figure perfectly. Her thick hair was pulled back in a simple low ponytail that exposed the full length and elegance of her neck. Her face was free of makeup except for light mascara and a subtle gloss on her lips. The look was unassuming but so fresh and different from what CC was used to that it took her breath away. "Wow. You look great. I don't think I've ever seen you in jeans."

Beth chuckled and then winked. "So I surprised you again?"

"Definitely."

"Good," she said with assurance as she gave CC a quick once-over. "And you look lovely, as always. Come in." She stepped aside to make room for CC to enter and closed the door behind her guest. Willow sat politely at the door, her tail wagging frantically as she waited to be greeted.

CC bent over to scratch the animal's muscular neck and looked around the room. If Beth's look had surprised her, her home was as inviting, simple and clean as she'd imagined. The front room combined a small L-shaped kitchen in its right corner, a dining area in its center and a living room on its left side. CC spotted a hallway behind the dining area that led to three doors she imagined were two bedrooms and a bathroom. The hardwood floors and the wood of the kitchen cabinets warmed up the house. The furniture was limited to essentials: a small, square wooden dining table with four chairs, a contemporary cream-colored leather sofa, a black reading chair and a sleek, low TV cabinet with several closed doors. A large square pillow tucked between the sofa and the reading chair served as Willow's bed. A vase filled with colorful wild flowers sat on the dining table. A few potted plants were scattered around the room and CC could guess from their healthy green leaves that the large front window provided them with plenty of light during the day. The wooden blinds were currently shut to give them privacy. No open shelves exposing dust-collecting objects, no area rug, not even a coffee table. CC appreciated the absence of clutter and immediately felt comfortable.

"I love your place. It's very you."

"Thank you. It's small, but it's all we need. Right Willow?" Willow wagged her tail again in response before she retreated to the living room and fell onto her bed with a loud thud followed by a heavy sigh.

"I guess we're not entertaining enough for her," CC said with a chuckle.

"I guess not, at least until we get dinner on the table. Then she'll be our best friend again, you'll see."

"I have no doubt. Speaking of dinner, here." She gave Beth the bottle of wine she was still holding in her hands. "It's supposed to go well with chili. I know you're not much of a drinker, but I think you'll like this one."

"Thank you, I'm sure it will be great. Have a seat, please. It's almost ready."

"I can smell it," CC said as she breathed in the sweet and spicy aromas. "It smells delicious, and I'm starving. What can I do to help?"

"I have everything under control, but you could open the wine if you don't mind. Glasses are over there."

CC reached the cabinet door Beth indicated and grabbed two glasses. "Wine opener?" CC asked while she was already opening a drawer to look for the tool. "Never mind, I found it."

They shared a smile, and CC wondered if Beth also shared her own thought that it was kind of odd yet very pleasant the way she already felt so at ease in Beth's environment. CC let the reflection linger as she started working on the bottle of Syrah.

Beth took cornbread muffins out of the oven and placed them in a bread basket. She then proceeded to ladle large portions of mouth-watering chili into two large bowls. As soon as dinner was on the table Willow bounced up from her bed and came to sit by CC's chair, staring at her with her big, black, pitiful puppy eyes. "Sure, now you love me, huh?"

"She won't stay as long as you don't..." Beth stopped mid-sentence when she saw CC slip a piece of cornbread to the dog. "Now you've done it, missy. You're stuck with her," she said sternly despite her mocking smile.

"I can deal with that," CC replied, dropping another piece of cornbread on the floor. They ate unhurriedly and enjoyed their conversation as much as their food. Willow eventually got bored and went back to her bed. CC had expected she would have a hard time getting Beth to drink one glass of wine so she was surprised when she kept refilling both of their glasses equally through dinner.

"It looks like I'm a bad influence on you," she teased when she emptied the bottle into Beth's glass.

"Oh Ciel, you really have no idea how bad I can be, do you?" Beth replied with daring aplomb. The intense gaze she threw under heavy eyelids caused a tingling sensation throughout CC's body.

Enjoying the playful provocation, CC decided to push further. "Who do you think you're kidding, Beth? You know nothing about being bad," she said in a low voice she didn't mean to be quite so raspy. Wine was having its effect on her as much as on Beth.

"Don't be so sure of yourself. You know I can be surprising," Beth offered, matching CC's huskiness and holding her gaze.

"Oh really? Name one bad thing you've done in your life." Beth looked down to her glass of wine and when she looked back up her eyes were filled with tears. CC immediately regretted pushing Beth. "Oh god, Beth. What's wrong? I was just playing, you know."

"I know, Ciel. I'm sorry. Your question just brought me back to the thing I'm the least proud of in my life."

CC reached across the table to cover Beth's hand with her own. "I'm sorry. We don't have to talk about it."

Beth turned her hand under CC's and laced their fingers. "I think I want to though," she said hesitantly.

CC rubbed Beth's hand with her thumb. "Okay. I'll be happy to listen," she whispered before offering her most tender and compassionate smile, filing away her shock at how serious the conversation had turned and her discovery that Beth might be less than perfect after all. She wanted nothing more than to be there for her friend.

"It's hard to admit it. Actually I never talked to anyone about it. You're right about me, you know. In general I take pride in always doing the right thing and I'm glad that's the way people see me, including you. But I've made at least one very bad decision in my life, and I want you to know about it, even if it means you might lose a lot of respect for me. Even if it might completely change the way you see me."

CC squeezed Beth's hand a little harder to encourage her. "It can't be that bad, Beth. Tell me."

Beth took a deep breath and closed her eyes before she finally let it out. "I had an affair with a married woman for over two years." Beth followed her revelation with a timid smile and waited for CC's reaction.

CC was torn. She had to admit that if another friend had told her the same thing she wouldn't have thought much of it. Infidelity was only too common. She didn't know if it was because of her own recent experience with Liz or if she was holding Beth to a whole different set of standards, but she was stunned. Her first reaction was to assume extenuating circumstances.

"How did it happen? You fell in love with her and then she told you she was married?"

"No Ciel. I knew she had a husband from the beginning. She warned me that all we could ever have was an affair. I went into it knowingly. I have no excuse whatsoever." She spoke determinately, leaving no room for mitigation.

"Wow," CC finally said. "I have to say you got me there. I wasn't expecting that at all."

"And?" Beth asked with apprehension as she took her hand out of CC's and started fidgeting nervously with her napkin. "You're disappointed, aren't you?"

"No, no, that's not it," CC answered quickly without taking the time to ask herself if she was, in fact, disappointed.

"What is it, then?"

CC looked into Beth's eyes and saw a condemned woman patiently waiting for her sentence, as if CC had any right to judge her. Realizing the importance of her opinion in Beth's eyes, CC took the napkin out of the grasp of her friend's nervous hand and held it in hers again. "I don't know exactly. But I don't like or respect you any less, Beth. It only makes you human. We all fuck up. You fucked up, that's all. And you regret it and I'm sure you wouldn't do it again, would you?"

"Never," Beth said before her voice broke and tears fell to her cheeks. CC stood up and walked around the table to give Beth a hug. Still in a sitting position, Beth wrapped her arms around CC's waist and held her tight, her face nesting into CC's stomach. "Thanks for not judging me."

"I have no right to judge you," CC replied as she moved her hand over Beth's ponytail, letting her fingers slide through the soft hair in a motion that soothed both women. "You must have loved her very much."

"I did," Beth confessed against CC's sweater. "I was stupid enough to think she'd leave him for me even though she kept telling me she wouldn't. It took two years for me to finally get it and a couple more months to end the affair. I wanted more and she couldn't give it to me."

"Tell me about her," CC prompted before she took Beth's hand and led her to the leather sofa. They sat sideways to face each other, and CC watched Beth's eyes light up at the memories that were rushing through her mind.

"She was African-American and a few years older than me. So beautiful. God, her body was out of this world." She giggled bashfully and bit her lip before she continued, "And so smart, so ambitious. She was a businesswoman. She would talk to me about her projects, and I swear it turned me on as much as her touch. I loved everything about her. Well, except for the fact that she couldn't face being gay and get out of her sham of a marriage."

A strange pang of jealousy hit CC, but she kept listening. The rumors had to be wrong. How could Beth have any interest in her after loving a woman who seemed so exceptional in every way? And more importantly, why was she suddenly comparing herself to that mysterious woman? Beth had stopped talking so CC decided to ask a question. "When did all of that happen?"

"Ten years ago. I'd just started at D&B..." Her voice trailed off before she cleared her throat and concluded, "Anyway, it took me years to get over that heartbreak, but I never got over how stupid I was to get involved in that situation in the first place. I knew it was wrong, and I did it anyway." She turned on the sofa as if she could no longer face CC. She was staring blankly at the TV when she added, "So you see, Ciel, I'm far from perfect. In fact, you're a much better person than I am."

CC accepted Beth's choice to stop talking about the affair. She'd heard enough about that wonderful woman, if she was honest with herself. She moved to the edge of the sofa to enter

Beth's peripheral vision before she attempted to lighten the mood.

"Yeah right. I'm no better than you, Beth. I'm bad to the bone. Did you know I used to smoke pot every morning before work? You better not mess with me." CC puffed her chest and squinted her eyes to look as mean as she could. When Beth burst out into laughter, she broke into a smile of her own, relieved her attempt at humor had succeeded.

"Of course I knew. Even if you hadn't smelled like a rock concert, your eyes would've been a dead giveaway. Do you really think I don't know a stoned look when I see one, Ciel?"

"Wait, you knew? But you never said anything."

"I'm not saying I liked it, but as long as I didn't see you smoke and you did your work, there was nothing I could do."

"I see. Well, I don't do it anymore. I quit at the same time I started running."

"I know. And I'm really glad you quit." Beth let her head fall onto the back of the sofa. She looked so much more relaxed. "You smell a lot better," she whispered.

"Thank you," CC whispered back. She let her own head rest against the back of the sofa and felt an urge to ask, "So, have you had other relationships since the affair?" She turned her head toward Beth without losing contact with the back of the sofa, waiting for an answer.

Beth turned her head in the same way so she was looking at CC in the eye when she answered, "No. It took years before I could even be interested in anyone else."

Holding Beth's deep gaze, CC dared, "But eventually you did get interested in someone else right?"

"Yes, I did." The hoarse whisper and the powerful look were too revealing for CC to keep ignoring the facts. It was true. Beth had gotten interested in someone else and that someone was her. The recognition warmed her inside, but when Beth moved slightly closer she panicked. She would have to deal with Beth's feelings for her and would need to examine her own, but she wasn't ready for any of that right now. It was too soon after

Liz and she'd had too much wine. So did Beth, for that matter. She stood up and walked toward the TV.

"So, what *Buffy* episode did you want to watch?"

If Beth was offended by CC's sudden withdrawal, she didn't let it show. "Any one you want. I have all the DVDs."

"Really? All seven seasons?"

"Yep. All of them."

"Then I guess we should start from the beginning."

Beth giggled and got up to set up the DVD. "You got it."

CC sat on one end of the sofa while Beth settled on her own side, and they watched a few episodes of Season One, discussing the characters and plots with enthusiasm. Eventually CC fell asleep on the couch. When she woke up with a stiff neck, it was still dark outside. Beth was no longer on the sofa, but in her place were a pillow and a blanket. CC laid her head on the soft pillow and covered herself with the blanket. She quickly went back to sleep, listening to the strangely comforting sound of Willow's light snoring.

CHAPTER FIFTEEN

CC took another deep breath of the cold, pure early November air. Walking with Beth and Willow on the wooden paths of Peebles Island State Park on this early Saturday morning, she had to admit Beth was right. This was exactly what she needed to alleviate some of the stress of the past few weeks. She'd started her new position as client relationship manager a few days after Jeff Hudson's departure and the transition had been very demanding. Not only was there a lot to learn, but some of Jeff's clients had lost faith in D&B because of Jeff's actions and CC felt pressure to turn things around quickly. She had to gain their confidence and she had to do it immediately. Joanna and the other managers were supportive, but the situation was extremely stressful nonetheless.

Beth had been there for her every step of the way. She was CC's sounding board when she needed advice and she always found encouraging words. She also made sure they kept to their running schedule. CC was convinced the exercise and Beth's friendship were keeping her sane. They'd shared several more dinners at Beth's house and were well into the third season of *Buffy the Vampire Slayer*. CC needed Beth in her life, that fact was not debatable.

"Thank you so much for thinking of this, Beth. I'd forgotten how beautiful this place is." Because of the near-freezing temperature, she had hesitated when Beth had suggested they explore Peebles Island instead of going for their usual run, but her jeans and fleece jacket sufficed to keep her warm, especially after twenty minutes of walking at a fast pace. The path that first took them through a dense forest was now lining a steep ravine and offered remarkable views of the Mohawk River and its impressive rapids. CC felt free and at peace.

"You're most welcome, Ciel. I haven't been here in years. I'm glad you came with us."

CC risked a sideways glance at Beth and recognized the longing that was appearing more and more often in the stunning green eyes. She chose to ignore it again and focused on the river instead. It had been over two months since her breakup with Liz and several weeks since the last email she'd received from her. She no longer cried herself to sleep every night; there were even days when she didn't think of Liz at all.

Yet the redhead was still ever so present. Like now. Like every time CC thought of the possibility of a relationship with Beth. On paper Beth was the perfect partner. She would treat her with respect and she would love CC the way she ached to be loved. She could feel it, knew it beyond the shadow of a doubt.

She even thought she could return Beth's love. Beth was easy to love, after all. She was intelligent, nurturing and yes, more and more attractive every day. But there was something missing. Something she couldn't describe. Some would call it a *je ne sais quoi* or perhaps the x factor. CC called it the Liz factor. The way she'd felt so alive, so powerfully stimulated in every possible way when in Liz's presence. It was like Liz had been her first high and she was now desperately chasing the dragon, looking for that same sensation.

She didn't feel that way with Beth. She wanted to, but it wasn't there, and she didn't know if she could settle for less, even though she realized her expectations were most likely unrealistic. It was all highly frustrating.

Her musings were interrupted when Beth put an arm in front of her to stop her from taking her next step. "Oh my god, look," Beth whispered as she pointed to the scene she wanted to share with CC. CC had been so preoccupied with her thoughts she hadn't realized that the path had led them back into the forest. She followed Beth's pointing finger and gasped when she saw the group of five white-tailed deer grazing in the woods no more than a hundred feet from them.

CC grabbed the arm Beth had used to stop her and squeezed it in her excitement. "Holy shit, they're gorgeous," she said as low as she could in her state of elation. Willow saw the deer almost at the same time and barked before Beth could stop her. The alerted deer immediately took off, and Beth and CC watched in awe as they leaped across the path and kept running until their white tails disappeared into the woods. "Wow! I can't believe we just saw this," CC exclaimed as she threw her arms around Beth's shoulders and pulled her into a euphoric hug.

Beth returned the hug and laughed her usual low chuckle. "I know! I've never seen that many together. It was…"

"Magical?" CC offered. She pulled away from the hug but left her hands on Beth's shoulders. She stared into her eyes, into the green she had not yet been able to identify. It was darker than emerald green but not quite as dark as forest green. It was absolutely beautiful, that much she was sure of. Was she really going to pass on someone as wonderful as Beth because of some elusive feeling she might never experience again? This moment really did feel magical, and it wasn't only because of the five white-tailed deer that ran in front of them. It was because she was sharing it with a phenomenal woman.

Beth's sudden sharp intake of air made CC aware that she'd moved closer to the taller woman and she felt Beth's hands on her hips. "Yes, magical," Beth murmured before she closed the remaining distance between them and pressed her lips against CC's. The deep moan that escaped Beth at the very first contact of their lips vibrated through all of CC's erogenous zones, from her neck to her nipples then made it all the way down to her stomach and her sex.

CC had never felt so much pent-up desire in one single moan. It communicated a profound need that she felt compelled to fulfill in any way she could. She took Beth's head between her hands and pulled her closer, urging the tentative lips to press harder against her own, inviting Beth to deepen the kiss, giving her permission. Beth's lips were soft and still hesitant, as if she had a hard time believing this was really happening. When CC parted her lips Beth moaned again and finally let her mouth take what was offered. CC felt Beth's tongue enter her mouth and explore it thoroughly, gliding delightfully against her own tongue. The next moan she heard was her own.

Encouraged, Beth wrapped her arms around her and held her so tight their breasts pressed together. This time their moans were simultaneous. Beth's assurance built up as their kiss intensified and soon CC melted in strong arms and whimpered as confident lips and tongue possessed her. When they had to force their mouths apart to catch their breath, Beth kept holding CC and her eyes, a whole new shade of green, searched CC's for any sign of regret.

CC's answer was another kiss, one that she initiated and controlled from beginning to end. It was her turn to taste Beth's mouth, to lick and nibble on Beth's lips, to cause sounds of pleasure for what she was doing to Beth and not only for giving her what she'd been wanting for so long. They kept kissing in the middle of the path for a long time and eventually their give-and-take became seamless. CC enjoyed every second of it. Beth was a wonderful kisser. She mentally added that trait to an already long list of great qualities and admitted to herself that sex with Beth would have to be mind-blowing.

She had to give this woman a chance, she simply had to. The damn "Liz factor" had failed her miserably in the end, and here she was kissing a woman who cared for her, who'd never lied to her, whose kisses left her quivering with pleasure and wet with want. She also felt safe in Beth's arms, something she'd never felt with Liz, something that had to make up for whatever what missing.

Willow grew impatient, pacing around them and obviously not understanding why they weren't walking. There was much more of this path to investigate and so many more odors to sniff. Beth laughed against CC's mouth and gave her another tender peck on the lips before turning her attention to Willow.

"Okay, okay beast. I get it." When Beth turned back to her, CC couldn't help but return the silly grin that was on her face. "I guess we should keep moving. Willow's going nuts and you look cold."

CC hadn't noticed, but she was shivering. Once again Beth seemed to know what she needed better than she did. "Yeah, I'm freezing. Let's go." She only grabbed Beth's hand to pull her forward onto the path, but when Beth didn't let go and instead laced their fingers together she didn't fight it because it felt nice. They walked the rest of the loop in complete silence, each in her own thoughts. They glanced at one another a few times and in time CC saw Beth's expression change. While she'd looked positively ecstatic right after their kiss, she appeared discernibly concerned by the time they got back to the parking lot. They reached Beth's car first. CC watched her open the back door to let Willow inside.

"Hey you, what's wrong?" she asked, leaning her back against the driver's door to keep Beth from opening it. CC put her hands on Beth's hips and pulled her toward her until their pelvises touched, a position that felt comfortable and brought a smile back on Beth's lips.

Beth placed one hand on CC's shoulder and the other on her chest, where she played with the zipper of the fleece jacket, her gaze focused on her fidgeting. "Nothing's wrong. It's just…"

CC brought her hand to Beth's chin and lifted her head to force eye contact. "It's just what?"

"I'm awfully scared what happened in the woods won't happen again, and I really, really want it to happen again." She whispered the last words, her eyes focused on CC's mouth.

CC felt the heat of her stare on her lips and swallowed hard before she spoke. "I want that too, Beth. Why wouldn't it happen again?"

"I don't know. Because your brain will thaw out eventually?" They both giggled for a few seconds, but the humor left Beth's eyes when she continued, "You will remember Liz."

"Oh Beth," CC said softly. "I can't say I've forgotten Liz because that'd be a lie. But I know she's not good for me, and I'll never go back to her. You, on the other hand, are very good for me." She grinned when she saw her declaration had made Beth smile. "And you're a damn good kisser, so I definitely want what happened in the woods to happen again, preferably in a warmer place." They laughed again and CC felt Beth relax against her.

"Does that mean you're willing to give us a chance?" Beth asked with more hope than apprehension.

CC took a deep breath before answering the question truthfully. "Yes, I really want to give us a chance." Beth conveyed her relief and satisfaction at CC's answer with another kiss. CC felt the weight of Beth's upper body pin her to the car as the kiss heated up. She didn't feel cold again until Beth drove away.

* * *

CC kept coming to work early even though her new position required her to stay at least until five p.m. every night. The early hours allowed her to study reports without being disturbed. She also didn't have the heart to ask Kayla to find another ride to work in the morning.

On the Monday following her excursion to Peebles Island with Beth, she walked toward the QA room with Kayla at seven thirty sharp. The official reason was that she needed to go over a specific report with Beth. The less official reason was that she couldn't wait to see her. She was surprised to find this giddiness in her and she enjoyed it very much. When they entered the QA room she was attacked by a strong smell of garlic mixed with something even more offensive she couldn't identify. "Phew! What the hell is that smell?"

"It's the new guy. Steve. It's disgusting isn't it? I swear the guy has the worst breath ever. It follows him around like a fucking cloud and stays in every room he walks into for hours.

I bet even his phone has bad breath. I can't stand this shit, CC. Please come back."

"Oh god. You know I can't come back but this is vile. Has Beth talked to him?"

"She has. I had to be there as a witness. That's a discussion you want to have with someone. 'Hey, buddy, you smell like crap. Do something about it.'"

"And it hasn't changed?"

"Obviously not. Good thing he's still on probation. I think Beth will get rid of him. The one good thing about Steve is that talking about his stench got me and boss-lady closer."

CC had to laugh at the comment. "Oh yeah? You bonded over his funk?"

"You bet your ass we did. Steve's foul odor and how much we miss you. That's what keeps us going."

"Aww, I'm touched."

"You should be, bitch." CC's gaze met Kayla's tiny, buzzed slits and they smiled. "I do miss you, baby girl."

"I miss you too, K."

The door to the QA room opened and Beth entered, carrying two coffees. She hadn't stopped bringing CC coffee every morning even after CC had convinced her she could manage her own breakfast now that she had adopted the good habits Beth had helped her develop.

"Oh god, that smell," Beth declared before she saw CC was in the room. "That's it, Kayla. He has to go today." She turned to Kayla to confirm her decision and finally saw CC standing by Kayla's chair. "Oh, good morning, Ciel."

"Good morning." The smiles they exchanged were sweet and flirtatious and entirely too revealing to share in Kayla's presence. She followed Beth to her cubicle where they couldn't be seen even though her dear friend could still hear them. CC cleared her throat and tried to sound serious. "I wanted to go over that report for AccBreezy if you have a few minutes. I have a meeting with them at nine and I'd like to give them a final count on the number of leads we'll credit them."

"Sure, let me print it out and we'll go over it right away." Beth hit the "print" button and walked to the printer located in a small adjacent room.

CC went back to Kayla's cubicle while she waited and heard her friend's evil snicker as she put on her jacket. "I'm going to smoke a cig, baby girl, but don't think for a minute you're fooling me. I know there's something going on between you and boss-lady and you'll tell me all about it later. That's a promise." She winked and exited the room as Beth was returning with her printed report.

When she noticed they were alone, Beth smirked at CC and playfully hit her shoulder with the report. "You know, I could have emailed you this report. I doubt there's anything in it a fancy client relationship manager such as you couldn't understand."

"I know," CC answered before letting her arms snake around Beth's waist and pulling her behind the safety of her cubicle wall. "But then I couldn't have done this." She raised her chin to reach Beth's lips and kissed her gently. Beth purred at the contact of their lips and returned the kiss with hunger. She let the report fall to the floor to thread her fingers through CC's hair and they kept kissing until they were both panting. CC straightened out her hair and bent down to pick up the report.

"See, I told you it would happen again," she said with a mischievous smile.

Beth's breathy chuckle was sexy and the invitation that followed even sexier. "What would you say about dinner at my place tonight?"

"I'd say abso-fucking-lutely. I have a meeting with Joanna at five though, so I'll be later than usual. Is that okay?"

"Of course. How did you say it? Abso-fucking-lutely?"

"That's right." She felt an instant blush on her neck and face. "You know, bad words sound really, really hot coming out of your pretty mouth. We'll have to explore that."

"Looking forward to it."

"Great. Have a good day, Ms. Andrews."

"You too." One more soft peck and CC was out of the QA room just in time for Kayla to come back from her smoke break and see how flushed she was.

She snickered again and shook her head. "Oh yeah, we need to talk. And soon."

Knowing there was no point denying anything, CC winked at her friend and mouthed, "Soon."

* * *

CC sat across from Joanna Dixon in an office that was barely larger than her own. The desk that separated them was modest and free of clutter. Yet there was no doubt she was sitting in the big boss's office. Joanna's presence was enough to make that point. It was in her straight and solid posture, in the way her facial expression never betrayed uncertainty, stress or even fatigue. Her quiet dominance was indisputable: she was in charge. Curtis Brown, cofounder of Dixon & Brown Communications, had already gone into retirement when CC started working for the company. But from what she heard, Joanna had been the only one in charge long before Mr. Brown's official departure. Tonight she wore another impeccable power suit and glanced at CC intermittently as she examined one report after another. Their meeting had started at five p.m. and it was now six o'clock. They'd discussed every client CC had taken over and were now reviewing the AccBreezy account, their largest client and one they could definitely not afford to lose. Joanna finally rested her eyes on CC after finishing her study of the report. "I see you offered to replace fifty leads for free?"

"I did," CC said with apparent confidence even as Joanna's questioning gaze made her unsure of her decision. "The truth is the number of unqualified leads Jeff sent them over the past twelve months is at least twice that, and I feel we owe our client retribution for the crap Jeff gave them. To be honest I think we're getting off easy with fifty leads, but Jake seemed very pleased with that offer."

Jake Lowell was the marketing director at AccBreezy and her main contact with the company. He was the man she needed to impress.

"What I'm trying to do, Ms. Dixon, is to get Jake to trust me and thus trust D&B again. I feel fifty leads is an investment that's well worth the expense if it keeps us from losing this account."

Joanna stared intensely into CC's eyes for what seemed like a few days and nights before a restrained smile finally appeared on her full lips.

"I agree, Ms. Charbonneau. You did very well. In fact, I think you should know that Mr. Lowell called me right after your meeting to tell me he was very satisfied with the way you've been handling things since you took over."

CC felt herself blush with pride at Joanna's words. "Thank you. That's good to know."

Joanna simply nodded. "That said, I wouldn't be a good businesswoman if I didn't ask you how you plan to minimize the costs of this necessary reparation. Looking at these reports I see we average ten hours to generate one lead. That's five hundred phone hours you're asking the company to eat, am I correct?"

"No, I assure you it will take less that that. You're right, we're averaging ten hours per lead. However if you look more closely at the report you'll see four of the phone reps who work on the AccBreezy campaigns average four hours per lead or less. If I can use these four reps for my replacement leads we could be done in two hundred hours or less. These four reps also generate quality leads. I know that from my experience in QA. So if I can use them, we'll limit not only the number of hours used but also the number of disqualifications."

Joanna smiled again and looked through the report to verify CC's information. "I see. Jimmy, Diana, Roberta and Sean. These are the reps you want, correct?"

"Yes. The problem is they're our top performers and if we use them on replacement leads we'll be left with less competent reps to work on the current campaigns, which brings me to my next point."

"Which is?"

"I need a few intensive training sessions not only with these reps but with their supervisors. I'm not talking about sitting in a conference room to go over the benefits of the software. I'm talking about role playing, listening to lead recordings and discussing what makes them good or bad. I'd also like to get QA involved. Beth already agreed. You see, Ms. Dixon, we can't afford to have only four great reps while a bunch of mediocre reps spend too many hours generating bad leads that don't meet our clients' expectations."

Joanna interrupted CC's rant with a raised hand. "You're preaching to the choir, Ms. Charbonneau. I like where you're going, but I will need you to come up with a very detailed plan. How many sessions? How long each session will take? What exactly will be covered in each session and who will be involved? I want you to come back to me with a formal proposal by next week. Do you think you can handle that?"

"Yes, absolutely."

"Great. I'm sure Ms. Andrews, or Beth as you call her, will be happy to help." CC thought she noted a hint of reproach in Joanna's voice when she mentioned Beth, but it quickly disappeared as she smiled and continued, "It seems you and Ms. Andrews have the same goals in mind and I plan on doing all I can to support you. We need to get everyone in this company to pay more attention to quality and I'm confident the two of you are the ones to do it. In the meantime I'll speak to the supervisors and you'll have your four reps to work on replacement leads starting tomorrow."

"Thank you, I appreciate it."

"You're welcome, Ms. Charbonneau. Is there anything else I can help you with at this time?"

"No, I think we covered everything."

"Very well." She paused but didn't make any dismissive gesture or declaration so CC remained seated. She'd never seen hesitation in Joanna's demeanor, but there was no other way to interpret the way she opened her mouth and closed it again a couple times before she finally spoke.

"There's one more thing. I think I've made it clear I don't pay much attention to the rumor mill in this place, but there's one that caught my attention recently." CC nodded and felt her body sink deeper into her seat. "It involves you and Ms. Andrews." CC nodded again, more sheepishly. She couldn't lie to the woman staring at her. "I trust the two of you to be discreet, Ms. Charbonneau."

"Of course," CC offered timidly.

Joanna cleared her throat and her gaze became more severe, almost threatening. Her smiles, even the most restrained of them, had all disappeared. "I also trust you to treat Ms. Andrews as well as she deserves to be treated. Beth and I have worked together for a very long time. I hold her in high regard and do not want to see her hurt. Am I making myself clear, Ms. Charbonneau?"

"Yes. You have my word."

"Fantastic. Have a great night, Ms. Charbonneau."

"You too." Joanna's nod and brief smile efficiently concluded the conversation, and the powerful woman had turned back to her computer before CC was out of her office.

* * *

CC sat in her own office for long minutes staring blankly at her computer screen. At first she didn't quite understand Joanna's warning words regarding Beth and their rumored relationship. She would have expected this kind of talk from Beth's family or even her best friend, but not from their boss. Then things started adding up. Joanna was a beautiful African-American woman. She was sexy, ambitious, intelligent. And very married. Beth had mentioned that her affair with a very similar woman had started not too long after she was hired at D&B. It didn't take a genius to figure out that the mysterious woman with whom Beth had an affair was the one and only Joanna Dixon.

How dare she? CC thought in sudden anger. How dare she warn CC about hurting Beth when she was the one who'd broken her heart all those years ago?

And then she understood. Like a family member, like a best friend, Joanna had warned CC because she loved Beth. She still loved her; it was obvious in her expression and in every one of her carefully chosen words.

The only question that remained was whether Beth knew about this undying love. She had to know. They worked together every day, met behind closed doors regularly. CC couldn't help but wonder if their meetings were always about business. Was there any chance their affair would or could ever rekindle? Worse, was there any way it had never really died in the first place? She couldn't believe Beth could hide something like that, but she'd been burned too deeply and too recently not to at least consider the possibility.

The lump that had lodged itself in her throat after her meeting with Joanna grew larger every second she kept staring at her computer screen. She grabbed her keys and exited her office. The building was dark except for the light coming out of Joanna's office. CC walked past the open door without even a glance in the woman's direction. She had to get to Beth's house.

* * *

Beth opened the door and CC was welcomed with a warm smile and a slow, gentle kiss before she could even take her jacket off. "I missed you. Dinner's almost ready. I hope you like pot roast."

"It sounds perfect and smells even better, thank you. And I missed you too."

CC thought she could get used to this kind of treatment after a day at work and hoped for the hundredth time since she'd left the office that she was being paranoid about Joanna's strange warning and what it might cover. Beth returned to the kitchen, and CC removed her boots at the door and hung up her coat in the tiny closet before she got on her knees to greet Willow. The Boxer's little knob of a tail wagged energetically, and when CC started scratching that magic spot behind her ears, she was rewarded with a wet kiss on the cheek.

"That's right, getting kisses from my two favorite girls. I'm a lucky woman."

"And don't you forget it," Beth said with laugh. CC was now used to seeing Beth in casual jeans and T-shirts but still felt a jolt of attraction every time. She wasn't sure if it was the way Beth's ass looked in jeans or the privilege of being one of the rare people to see her dressed that way. Most likely both. She couldn't help but think that Joanna had seen Beth that way too. But when was the last time? Beth caught CC staring and winked as she fixed two plates of pot roast, mashed potatoes and a green salad. "So? How did your meeting go?"

CC got up from the floor and joined Beth in the kitchen. She placed a soft kiss on Beth's neck as she walked behind her to get to the sink where she washed her hands. "It went well. Joanna agreed with my plans and even said it would be fine if you helped me put a formal proposal together for the training sessions. Did she talk to you about that?"

"No, but Joanna knows I'll help you. She knows I'll get behind any kind of initiative to promote quality in that place. It's long overdue." CC watched for something in Beth's expression as she answered. Some kind of clue or hint. What kind, she didn't even know, and she suddenly saw the foolishness inherent in her own behavior. She needed to come clean with her fears and stop playing games. She grabbed a plate of food and followed Beth, who was already sitting at the small dining table with her own plate.

"Joanna said something else about you. It was kind of weird."

Beth was about to take a bite of food when CC spoke and stopped the fork just an inch from her mouth before returning it to her plate. She seemed nervous when she asked, "What?"

"Well, she said she heard rumors about us and wanted to make sure we were discreet."

"Oh...Well, that makes sense. What did you say?"

"I said we would be of course, but then she went on telling me I better make sure I treat you well or else."

Beth's blush was instantaneous. First CC thought it was caused by embarrassment, but when Beth spoke she realized there was definitely some anger in her coloring. "She what? Did she actually threaten you, Ciel?"

"No, I don't think so. I don't remember her exact words, Beth, but it was clear she was asking me not to hurt you."

"She's got some nerve."

"That's what I thought too. It's weird, isn't it?"

Beth took a deep breath and reached across the table to cover CC's hand with her own. "Yes, it's weird, but there's a reason." Another deep sigh. "Ciel, the only reason I didn't tell you before was because I promised her I would never tell anyone, but if she's going to threaten you with stupid warnings I think you should know where it's coming from. Remember when I told you I had an affair with a married woman?"

CC immediately grabbed Beth's hand between both of hers and squeezed gently, relieved that the truth was coming out so easily. "Yes, I remember. It was Joanna, wasn't it?" Beth nodded. "I figured as much after what she said tonight. I think she still loves you, Beth." It hurt to say it, but CC had to, just in case Beth didn't know. Just in case it could change anything. Because if there was any chance it could, CC needed to know now.

"She might still love me, but it doesn't matter, Ciel. I told you the reason why I put an end to the affair was because I wanted more than she could offer. It wasn't because she stopped loving me or I stopped loving her. If I hadn't broken us up, we'd probably still be having an affair. That's what she wanted. But I couldn't do it anymore."

"And after you broke up all those years ago," CC hesitated. She didn't want to sound accusatory, but she had to ask, "You never, you know, went back? I mean, nothing ever happened again between the two of you? Even though you see each other every day at work?"

Beth understood the weight of the question and with the hand that wasn't trapped between CC's she caressed her anxious lover's cheek. "Never," she whispered with a reassuring smile. "She tried a few times in the beginning, but there was no going back for me. Then a couple of years ago, when she noticed I was developing feelings for someone else, she tried again. She even said she would consider getting a divorce if I gave her another chance."

"Really?"

"Yes, really."

"But wasn't that what you wanted?"

"It was at one point, yes, but she was years too late."

"Because you were falling for someone else?" CC's voice was small, her heart beating too loud. She held her breath as Beth stood up and walked around the table to sit in her lap. She felt the weight of Beth's arms on her shoulders and the rest of her body on her thighs like a security blanket and wrapped her own arms around the woman's hips.

"Because after the very first day you spent in QA, Ciel Charbonneau, I only had eyes for you." Beth confirmed her declaration with a smoldering kiss. CC couldn't believe she'd doubted this woman's loyalty. She couldn't believe it had taken her two years to notice the beauty of her heart, the sexiness of her body and the strength of her devotion. She let the hungry lips devour her mouth and moaned when it moved to her neck. A wet tongue laved her collarbone at the same time Beth's lower body shifted to straddle her. She moaned again, feeling the heat of Beth's center through her jeans. Needing to feel the warmth of skin, she slid her hands under Beth's T-shirt to caress her back before sliding beneath the waist of tight jeans to her backside. By then Beth was rocking lasciviously in her lap; CC helped the movement with her hands firmly holding both ass cheeks.

"I've wanted you for so long," Beth growled, stretching CC's T-shirt to kiss the soft flesh on top of her breast, just above her bra. CC felt the depth of Beth's want and anticipation, and she suddenly stopped massaging Beth's backside and took her hands out of her jeans.

There was too much pressure. She didn't know how she could meet Beth's expectations and not disappoint her after two long years of whatever fantasies she might have had, but she was abruptly convinced it couldn't be on a chair, in a dining room. It couldn't be so soon after she doubted Beth's loyalty. It couldn't be after the realization that Liz's betrayal was still so raw that it had made her question the most honest woman she'd ever met. It couldn't be now. Beth was still rocking against her and exploring every inch of exposed skin with her lips and tongue.

"Beth, wait," she said softly.

Beth stopped moving her hips and sighed before she let her head fall heavily onto CC's shoulder, obviously frustrated. When she raised her head to look into CC's eyes, however, she smiled. Her cheeks, neck and chest were flushed with desire. "What's wrong?" she asked with slightly more tenderness than apprehension.

"Nothing's wrong. I want you too, Beth, I really do. But I think we should take it slow. I really like you, and I don't want to mess up anything."

Beth chuckled before she pressed her lips against CC's in a kiss that was almost chaste. She sighed with resignation before she spoke. "Okay, I get it. I've been waiting for you for two years, Ciel. So you have to understand that things have already been very, very, excruciatingly slow for me."

They both giggled at the declaration before Beth captured CC's gaze with green eyes so full of affection that the next words seeped through CC's body like liquid warmth.

"That said, I'll keep waiting for as long as it takes for you to finally catch up with me."

CHAPTER SIXTEEN

CC finished drying the last pan and put it back in its place in the low cupboard by the oven. She still knew where everything went in her parents' small kitchen. Marie had cooked their Thanksgiving meal and had retired to the family room with a cup of tea, leaving Charles and CC to clean up. It was tradition. Charles then lit a fire in the fireplace of the cozy family room and began the task of rolling a marijuana cigarette.

"I know you quit, baby, but you won't mind if we do, will you?"

"Of course not, Dad. In fact I think I'll join you. It wouldn't be Thanksgiving without it. Some families have pumpkin pie; we have Mary Jane."

Marie laughed out loud and CC joined her on the couch, laying her head on her mother's lap. Marie immediately started playing with her daughter's hair like she'd done since CC was a little girl.

"Thanks for cooking, Mom. It was delicious and I ate too much as always."

"We all did, honey. It's part of the fun. Now tell us more about Beth. I still can't believe you've had a new girlfriend for weeks and we're just hearing about her."

CC had told her parents about her relationship with Beth over dinner. Of course they were very happy for her. Of course they wanted to meet Beth right away. CC couldn't help thinking that was part of the reason why she hadn't mentioned her new relationship before today. Her parents would have insisted that Beth come to Thanksgiving dinner and CC wasn't sure she was ready for that. When Beth had mentioned she was going to spend the holiday weekend visiting her family in Buffalo she'd been a little relieved. She knew if she'd asked Beth to stay she would have, but CC didn't ask.

Charles lit up the joint and passed it to his wife, who took a hit before passing it to her daughter. CC inhaled the smoke and enjoyed its taste. She hadn't smoked marijuana since that late summer night with Kayla and Damon, but she didn't feel guilty tonight. Smoking with her parents on a night like this was different from the smoking habit she once had. It was a special occasion, and she appreciated this joint like others would a glass of champagne on New Year's Eve. "I told you everything, Mom. She's amazing, and you'll meet her soon, I promise."

Marie took another hit before she looked at CC with that all too familiar "I see through your bullshit" look.

"You've told us almost everything, CC, but you're keeping the most important part to yourself, as you always do."

CC sat up on her end of the couch, putting some distance between herself and Marie. "Mom, please don't. You're right okay. I'm still working through some stuff, but I really don't want to talk about it."

"Some stuff about Liz, I assume?"

"Mom, please let it be."

Charles snorted a laugh as he breathed out the smoke he'd been holding in. "When have you known your mother to let things be, baby? She'll torture you all night so you might as well rip off the Band-Aid and get it over with."

Marie laughed in turn and CC was forced to admit defeat.

"Okay, okay. Yes, I still think about Liz. It's not that I want her back though. I'm really happy with Beth. She's wonderful and I know we're great together."

"But there's something in the way you felt about Liz that you can't find again with Beth."

CC sighed with exasperation. "Isn't it bad practice in your line of work to put words into your patient's mouth?"

"But you're not my patient, Ciel. You're my daughter. I know you. So am I wrong?"

"No, of course not. You're one hundred percent right."

Charles kept the joint and relaxed in the large recliner as the two women repositioned themselves to face each other on the couch. "Okay, so tell me about whatever it is you had with Liz that you can't find with Beth."

"It's hard to explain, Mom. I'd never felt it before and I'll probably never feel it again. It was like every nerve in me lit up around Liz, like every part of me was on fire when she was around. My mind, my body, my heart. Nothing else existed but her."

"And it's not like that with Beth?"

"No. It's great, not that...intense? I don't know the right word for it."

"Out of control?"

"Yeah, maybe. I was powerless, Mom."

"And that's a good thing?" the question came from Charles, which surprised both women.

"I don't know. Isn't it?" CC asked sincerely.

Charles had gone back to his silence, and Marie was the one who answered.

"It can be, honey. But what is important here is what you think. Do you think it's impossible to be truly in love without feeling out of control the way you did with Liz?"

"I don't know, Mom. I feel wonderful with Beth. I feel loved, safe, and I know I love her too." She was shocked at her own proclamation. It was the first time she said the words out loud.

"But I can't help feeling like I'm not being fair to her if I can't give her that all-consuming, crazy, out-of-control kind of love I gave Liz."

"Have you ever thought maybe the kind of love you have for her is exactly what she wants from you?" Marie's question wasn't one that needed an answer. They shared a smile and were startled by Charles' voice when he spoke again.

"I know you probably don't want my opinion, but I'm your dad and I'll give it to you anyway. It seems to me the kind of love you and Beth share is the real thing, baby. That shit you had with Liz, it can only hurt you. Trust me, if you want to feel out of control again, just drive up to Great Escapes and get on a roller coaster. Your wallet will pay for the thrill, not your heart."

CC laughed at her dad's metaphor and Marie suggested, yet again, that CC should talk to Dr. Simmons. "He'll help you sort everything out," she repeated. This time CC promised she'd make an appointment.

* * *

CC sat on her couch with Gerri Hill's latest romance novel, determined to enjoy a little alone time in her own house for the first time in days. She'd slept in her old room at her parents' house the night before, too buzzed to drive home after only three hits of the marijuana cigarette. She was definitely out of that habit and she was glad. After breakfast she'd gone for a run by herself and now, at eleven a.m., she was showered and ready to relax. She tried to focus on her book, but her mind kept going back to her conversation with her parents. They'd helped her shed some of her guilt about the feelings she had for Beth. Feelings that were growing stronger every day. Feelings that she needed to stop comparing to those she'd felt for Liz. Their love was different, but it was real.

She lay down on the couch with the open book resting on her chest. God, she was so ready to see Beth again and be with her without that stupid guilt that had weighed her down since their first kiss on Peebles Island. She was so ready to make love to her and give herself to her. Did Beth really have to stay in Buffalo until Sunday?

She smiled to herself. If Beth could wait two years she surely could wait two days. Beth deserved some time with her family and she wouldn't ask her to come home early. She jumped up when her cell phone rang, sending the book that was on her chest flying to the floor.

"Hello?"

"Hi Ciel." Beth. Her voice was low, almost shy.

"Hey you. I was just thinking about you. Are you having fun?"

"Yeah, but I was thinking about you too. I was missing you pretty badly, actually."

CC lay back down on the sofa and licked her lips. She didn't care if Beth was whispering only so no one could hear her. It was sexy as hell and it did things to her. Wonderful things. She used the same breathy type of voice to answer even though she was alone in her loft. "I miss you too, Beth. In fact I was talking about you last night when I was with my parents."

"Oh yeah?"

"Yeah. I even told them something I feel kind of bad about. Something I should have told you first." Her voice trembled.

"What is that?"

"I told them that I love you." CC heard a gasp on the other end of the line and kept talking. "It just came out and I'm really sorry you weren't the first one to hear it, but it's true, Beth. I love you."

"I love you too." A soft moan traveled from the phone through CC's skin. Then a loud voice called Beth's name. "Shit, I have to go, Ciel. They're waiting for me. I'll see you on Sunday. Bye."

"Bye." CC hung up the phone and couldn't help the grin on her lips. She picked up the book that was on the floor and placed it on the coffee table. There was no sense trying to read now. Her brain was too full of what Sunday might bring. It would be quite a reunion, she was certain of it.

Deciding to email Beth some of her thoughts, she turned on her laptop. She browsed through her inbox and quickly got rid of the junk. No, she wouldn't need Viagra and certainly not a larger penis. She laughed out loud. And then she saw it. An email from Liz with "Happy Thanksgiving" as the subject line.

* * *

CC walked past Damon and started pacing in front of the brown sectional, leaving him standing at the front door. Kayla sat in her usual spot. Judging by the thick cloud of smoke in the room, they'd just finished a blunt. Kayla and Damon exchanged an amused glance as he sat down next to her and they resumed watching CC. Her face was red, her fists so tight her knuckles were white. When Kayla finally spoke, she had a hard time not laughing.

"Are you gonna tell us what the fuck is going on, baby girl? Or are you gonna keep pacing until you burn holes through our carpet?"

"It finally happened, K. I'm officially pissed off," CC offered through clenched teeth.

Kayla clapped her hands and allowed herself to laugh briefly at the announcement. "About fucking time."

"What the hell did it take?" Damon asked before adding, "Sit down and tell us, girl. You're making me dizzy."

"None of it was real. None of it, damn it," CC mumbled more for herself than for her friends, still pacing.

"Enough, CC. Sit the fuck down right now and start from the beginning before I slap you." Kayla's voice finally got through to CC. She stopped moving and looked at the couple before she slouched onto the sectional. Damon fetched a bottle of water out of the fridge, handed it to her and then sat back down next to Kayla.

"Thank you." She gulped down half the bottle and started explaining. "I got an email from Liz. She's still in therapy. She says she's doing much better."

"Okay, sounds good so far. So what got you so riled up?" Kayla asked.

"She apologized for putting me through all the shit she put me through. Said she had no business getting involved with a nice woman like me when she didn't know how to love. She admitted she used me and asked for forgiveness." CC started crying and wiped her tears violently with the back of her hand, letting out a deep growl. Kayla and Damon looked at each other, puzzled.

"I'm sorry, CC. Obviously you're very angry about it all, but I don't get it. It seems to me like Lezzy McCrazy's finally doing the right thing. I didn't think she had it in her. Just sayin'."

"You don't understand, K. The one thing I still believed was that Liz did really love me. But it was all lies, all of it. She didn't even really love me because she wasn't capable of it. Don't you see what that means?" She didn't wait for Kayla's answer. "It means I've been torturing myself, feeling guilty, questioning my relationship with Beth, all that for something that was never real in the first place. It means I'm a complete idiot, K. She made a complete fool of me from beginning to end. I never thought I could say it, but right now I really hate that bitch with everything I've got. But most of all I hate myself. God, I'm so mad at myself." CC only stopped talking when her sobbing made it impossible for another word to come out.

"Wait a minute, baby girl. Stop this right now." Kayla moved next to CC and held her friend. CC let Kayla pull her face against her ample bosoms and watched the long fingernails, painted black with silver stars on the tips, as Kayla's hand moved up and down her arm in a soothing motion. "None of this is your fault, CC. The bitch is totally fucked up and she fucked you over good and hard, but that doesn't mean it wasn't real to you. Your feelings were real, your pain was real. It was all real to you, baby girl."

"But I almost missed my chance with Beth over it," CC said against Kayla's breasts.

"But you didn't. Boss-lady's crazy about you and you're crazy about her. And now that you're properly pissed off, I'm telling you that bitch will finally be out of your life for good and you can really move on. You'll see." Kayla held CC and rocked her gently for as long as the tears kept falling while Damon looked at his girlfriend with pride.

Once the crying finally stopped, CC took a deep breath and let it out, then broke free of Kayla's embrace. With a tentative smile, she took her friend's hand in hers and looked at her through what she knew were red-rimmed, burning blue eyes. "Thank you, K," she said softly. Then her smile became more of a smirk and she winked before she added, "You're pretty good at this consoling stuff, you know, for a tough girl."

"I know right? She'd make a good mama. She's got the boobs for it, that's for sure," Damon added with a wink of his own.

"Yep, that's for sure," CC confirmed, expecting the slap Kayla immediately gave her shoulder.

"You're such assholes, the both of you," Kayla replied before she started snickering. "Don't get used to it," she told CC before turning to Damon. "And don't you get any ideas about babies. No kid of yours is gonna suck on these tits. Ever."

* * *

Later that evening CC was back in her own loft, sitting on the window seat of her living room, gazing absently outside. She found herself surprisingly calm. She'd gone to see Kayla when the rage over Liz's email hit her because she knew Kayla would be the best person to be around in such a state of mind. She expected her friend to support her in her rant and she was ready to hear what a "crazy, fucking asshole Liz was, just sayin'". She thought they would have it all out in a bitching contest; that was exactly what she needed. Or so she thought.

Instead Kayla had been reassuring and—she hated to admit it—wise. Kayla had been right all along. CC needed to get angry at Liz, and now that she had done she felt liberated. Perhaps not completely free yet, but definitely closer to it. Free enough to look forward to seeing Beth on Sunday. Liz might still occupy some parts of her brain, but she would no longer be a part of her relationship with Beth. That was a promise she made to herself, a promise she knew she could keep.

She looked down at the joint she'd left next to her on the window seat. She'd refused to smoke with Kayla and Damon, but they'd insisted that she leave with a joint to enjoy once she was home alone. *Why not?*, she thought. She'd made a salad for dinner, had taken a bath, and now she was sitting here alone in her flannel pajamas. She didn't have anywhere to go and she wanted to relax.

As she mused about where she might have stored a lighter, she was startled by the buzz of the intercom. She looked down on the street, and her heart skipped a beat when she recognized Beth's car parked in front of her building. She let out an excited yelp and ran to the intercom to let Beth in.

"Oh my god, I'm so happy you're here. Come on up." She opened the door and stood in the doorway, staring at the elevator. It took forever. She suddenly remembered her snowflake-decorated flannel pajamas and the fact she wasn't wearing a bra or underwear. She didn't care. By the time the doors of the elevator finally opened and Beth appeared in front of her, she was smiling so much her cheeks hurt. Beth wore yoga pants and a sweatshirt. Her ponytail looked like it was still wet, as if she was just out of the shower. Her deduction was confirmed when she walked into Beth's open arms and smelled the fresh, familiar scent of her citrus soap.

CC nuzzled the long neck and breathed her in before she spoke.

"What are you doing here? I thought you were spending the weekend in Buffalo."

CC stepped out of Beth's arms and grabbed her hand to pull her inside the loft. She closed the door behind them and finally noticed how frazzled and anxious Beth appeared.

"I couldn't wait that long. I had lunch with my family and told them I had to go back home. I drove four hours to my house, fed Willow, showered, and here I am."

"Oh sweetheart," CC said softly as she put her arms back around Beth's waist, letting her hands caress her sides before resting them on her lower back. "I'm very happy you're here, but what was the rush? And why the hell aren't you wearing a jacket? It's freezing outside." She pulled Beth closer to her and rubbed up and down her back.

"I don't feel cold," Beth said flatly. She put her hands on CC's shoulders and held her at arm's length, staring at her as if she was looking for some information CC was holding from her. "I couldn't wait to see you, Ciel. Not after what you said this morning."

"What?" CC asked before she realized what Beth was referring to, and she felt a blush heat up her face. "Oh, I see."

"Yeah. Do me a favor okay? Next time you make a declaration like that, something I've been dreaming of hearing for over two years, please don't do it over the phone when I'm four long, torturous hours away from you. I've been going crazy thinking you might change your mind before I could even get to you. So have you?"

At CC's puzzled look, Beth asked again, "Have you changed your mind?"

"What? No. Of course not, silly. Why the hell would I change my mind?"

"I don't know. It could happen."

Beth took a deep breath as CC took her face in her hands and smiled tenderly. "Beth, I love you. I'm sorry I told my parents first. I'm sorry I told you on the phone first. But I'm not going to change my mind and I will keep telling you for as long as you want to hear it so you didn't have to leave your family and drive four hours to hear it."

"Yes, I did. That's all I could think about. You have no idea what this means to me, Ciel." The way Beth's eyes welled up with tears gave CC a clue. "Please say it again," she pleaded in a whisper.

"I love you," CC said again before brushing her lips against Beth's. She moved her mouth lower and kept her lips so close to the tender skin of Beth's neck as she murmured that each word became a kiss. "I love you. I'm going to keep telling you, and right now I'm going to show you."

She gave in to the urge to move her hands under Beth's sweatshirt and over her naked back. She hummed against Beth's neck when she realized she was not the only one not wearing a bra, but the low growl that escaped from Beth when CC's hands made contact with her skin overpowered any other noise in the loft.

CC was shocked when Beth took her hands out from under her sweatshirt and held her wrists above her head, pinning her to the back of the door with a strength she didn't expect. The sudden, surprising domination left her instantly wet and breathless.

"Are you saying you're ready to make love, Ciel?" The question was asked in a voice so hoarse, so filled with need, and the green glare was so intense that all CC could do was nod her answer. "Because if you're ready, my love, you should know I have had two long years to imagine ways to show *you* how *I* feel."

When Beth released CC's hands, CC quickly placed them on Beth's shoulders to maintain her balance when Beth took a firm hold of her backside and lifted her off the floor, forcing CC to wrap her legs around her hips. They leaned heavily against the door as Beth started grinding her pelvis into CC in slow, agonizing circles. "I'm going to make love to you, and I'm going to fuck you. And then I'll start over and do both at the same time, until there's no doubt in our minds that your body's finally mine, Ciel. All mine."

"Oh god, yes." CC was overwhelmed. Beth's sex moving against her own felt wonderful even through their clothing, but it was nothing compared to the assertiveness of her words. *Beth said "fuck," for fuck's sake.* "Fuck yes."

"Later, my love, you'll get your turn to touch me. But right now, if you really want to show me you love me, you'll let me do everything I've wanted to do for way too long. Will you?"

"Yes." And then she understood. The way her sex throbbed with want, the way blood rushed through her veins and her breath caught with every one of Beth's words, it was all from feeling so wanted. So clearly, undoubtedly, deliciously wanted.

"Put me down. Let me show you." Her request was soft but assured.

Beth carefully let CC touch the ground and move from the door. She let CC take her hand and followed her to the bedroom. She let CC guide her to the bed where she sat. She tried to follow again when CC moved away from her, but CC stopped her with a raised hand. "Stay right there. Just look at me."

Beth obeyed and nodded. A few feet in front of her, just out of reach, CC started to undress. Slowly. It was not a striptease. There was no music, no sensual dancing involved. It was more like an unveiling. Like a heavy cloak falling off a prized painting.

First she unbuttoned the top of her flannel pajamas and let it fall down her shoulders to the floor. She grinned when Beth gasped at the sight of her breasts. And when Beth bit her bottom lip in that way that drove CC crazy, she was tempted to walk to the bed and kiss her, press her breasts against her and let her have them. She wanted them; there was no doubt about that. CC felt empowered knowing that and chose to keep her distance and continue revealing herself.

She slipped her thumbs in the waistband of her pajamas, causing Beth to start to move toward her. CC raised her hand to stop her again. "No. Not yet. Just look. Look at me."

When Beth sat down and CC was certain she wouldn't move, she brought her hands back to her pajama pants and lowered them until a subtle shake of her hips sufficed to send them down to the floor. She stood there, in front of Beth, completely naked. "Look at me," she repeated in a breath. She turned to reveal her behind before facing Beth again. "It's all yours. Only yours," she added.

"You're so beautiful, Ciel. So lovely. Please, let me move now. Let me touch you."

CC slowly walked to the bed, closing the distance between them. She took Beth's hands and brought them to her breasts, pressing their palms onto her erect nipples. "It's all yours, Beth. Take it. You don't have to wait anymore."

That was all the permission Beth needed to pull CC to the bed and get on top again, in every possible way. CC was left alone on her back only for a few seconds while Beth got rid of her own clothes and then she felt the weight of Beth's body on her own.

Beth started massaging CC's breast with her hand. She held one nipple between her thumb and index finger and studied it. "It's perfect," she said softly. "Darker than I imagined. Your skin is so light I thought your nipples would be light pink, but this is perfect, like the color of your hazelnut coffee with cream."

CC moaned at the appraisal. She opened her legs and wrapped them around Beth's hips, pulling her closer. She'd never wanted someone inside her so much. She'd given herself to Beth, had granted her full access to her heart and body, and that gift had left her sex open, wet, ready and desperate to be filled by Beth.

Beth didn't seem to share the same sense of urgency. She began a slow exploration of CC's body with her lips and tongue, starting with her neck before moving back to her breasts. CC tried to focus on Beth's lips around her engorged nipple, on the tongue that flicked at it expertly, but her attention kept going back to the soft curls of Beth's sex caressing her own hairless, dripping lips. She raised her hips to push harder into Beth, panting. Out of control. Powerless.

There it was, that feeling she thought she wouldn't experience with Beth. Except it was better. It was not scary or dangerous. She was out of control, yes, but in the most delightful way. She whimpered and suddenly Beth's mouth was on hers, kissing her and then murmuring, "What is it, my love? Tell me what you want."

"I need you inside me. God, Beth, please fuck me now." CC saw Beth grin and felt two fingers plunge easily into her. Her eyes slammed shut and she screamed from pleasure. "Yes, that's it. More, please."

Beth added another finger and went deeper. She stayed there, twisting her fingers inside CC, reaching every spot that felt so good. Beth was now straddling one of CC's thighs, coating her skin with thick wetness. She contracted every muscle in her thigh, encouraging Beth to ride her, to experience her own pleasure.

"I'm going to make you come, Ciel," Beth panted as her three fingers drove her closer and closer to orgasm. "And I'm going to come with you."

CC felt Beth's breath on her mouth: the woman so deep inside her must have been staring at her when she made that sweet promise. CC opened her eyes and connected with Beth's green ones. They gazed at each other, their breathing becoming heavier and heavier. Beth pressed her thumb against CC's clitoris and the climax took over her body. Beth kissed her as she cried, moaned and growled into her mouth. She stayed inside her without moving her fingers until the last spasm. Then, removing her fingers, she started caressing her clitoris, letting it slide between her two middle fingers.

CC felt another orgasm build up and looked at Beth with awe. "Oh, fuck, I'm coming again. God, this feels so good."

Only when CC started trembling with her second orgasm did Beth start moving faster against her thigh, bringing herself to climax. Their bodies writhed and squirmed with pleasure as they rode their orgasms. Finally Beth let herself fall heavily onto the bed, her arm resting on CC's stomach, her head on her shoulder, chuckling softly as her breathing slowly came back to normal.

"What's so funny?" CC asked. Her own breathing was still erratic, every nerve of her body still hypersensitive.

"Nothing. I'm just very, very happy." She kissed CC's shoulder and gently bit her flesh. "And so not done with you."

* * *

They'd gone to sleep in CC's bed after hours of lovemaking, more exhausted than satiated. CC woke up and looked at the clock. It was after four in the morning. They'd slept for over an hour. She still needed a lot more sleep, but she felt rested enough to turn the tables on Beth and explore the body that had brought her so much joy in the same way Beth had explored hers.

She turned around with a mischievous smile, but Beth wasn't in bed. She was about to get out of bed and look for her when the naked woman sat down next to her on the bed, her hands behind her back. Her grin was so wicked CC could not help but chuckle.

"There you are. I kind of freaked out when I woke up and didn't find you. Where have you been, naughty girl? And what's behind your back?"

"Well, I went to the bathroom and as I walked past your living room window I saw that it's snowing so I watched the snow fall for a little bit, thinking about you."

"You stood in the nude in front of my living room window? You really are naughty, aren't you? Now show me what you're hiding behind your back."

CC reached out for Beth's arm, but Beth moved out of her reach. "Okay, I'll show you. I found it on your window seat, actually." CC remembered the joint before Beth brought her hand right in front of her face and opened it, revealing the tightly rolled cigarette. "Did you start smoking again, Ciel?"

Beth asked the question casually, almost playfully, but CC noted a touch of worry in her voice. She sighed heavily before she answered. "No, I swear I didn't. I went to Kayla's yesterday and she sent me home with this joint. I did smoke with my parents on Thanksgiving because it's kind of a tradition. I know it's weird, but it happens when you're raised by hippies." She was slightly relieved and smiled when Beth chuckled at the revelation. "But before that I hadn't smoked since the summer. I promise. I know you don't like it." CC lowered her eyes, looking like a child about to be punished.

Beth laughed at the sheepish look and kissed CC on the lips. "Cheer up, Ciel. I'm not the weed police. I wouldn't like it if you smoked every day and I sure don't want you to start coming to work buzzed again, but I don't care if you smoke with your parents or with Kayla once in a while. Just be honest about it and we won't have a problem okay?"

"Okay," CC agreed.

Beth brought the joint to her nose and took a deep breath, taking in the aroma with a smirk on her mouth. "God, it's been at least fifteen years since I've smoked one of these. I didn't think I'd see one again at my age."

A shiver passed through CC's body at the brand new opportunity presenting itself. "First of all, Ms. Andrews, thirty-six is definitely not too old for a buzz. Second of all, you have no idea how much you just turned me on telling me that you did smoke weed at one point in your life."

"Oh really?" Beth asked huskily, her mouth getting temptingly closer to CC's.

"Really."

"Then what would you say if I told you that the one thing I remember most about smoking weed is that it made me terribly horny?"

"I'd say let me get a lighter right now." CC jumped out of bed and Beth burst out laughing before she followed.

They didn't bother getting dressed before they smoked in front of the open living room window. They shared a thick blanket that they wrapped over their shoulders and sat snugly on the window seat. As CC had predicted, Beth coughed up all of the smoke on her first tries, but she was finally able to hold some smoke in. It didn't take much before her eyes became glassy, bloodshot, tiny slits. They hadn't even smoked half the joint, but CC put it out. She wanted Beth relaxed and aroused, not passed out on the floor.

Beth giggled uncontrollably as CC grabbed her hand and pulled her to the bedroom. She laughed even more when CC pushed her onto the bed and she fell on her back. When CC covered her with her nude body and pushed her tongue into her mouth, however, all laughter disappeared, replaced with raw hunger. Beth grunted into CC's mouth and reached around her to her ass, but CC took hold of her wandering hands and placed them on the pillow above Beth's head.

"No. It's my turn now. You just lie there and feel. Okay?" Beth nodded and bit her bottom lip. "You're going to feel so good, Beth. Just enjoy it." CC raised to her hands and knees and placed one knee between Beth's legs, brushing over the soft pubic hair but not putting any pressure where Beth needed it. Supporting herself on her knees and one hand, she used all five fingertips of her other hand to gently rake the length of Beth's body, from her shoulder to the middle of her chest and her stomach, avoiding her sex on purpose to continue to her thigh.

CC watched as Beth shivered under her touch. She knew Beth would push her pelvis against her knee to find the pressure she needed and she smiled when she did. Then she moved her knee back an inch, just out of reach. "Relax, we'll get there. But there's much more to feel before then. Can you feel this?" She used the back of her hand to go back up the same path her fingertips had traced.

"Yes, I feel it. I feel so much. Like you're touching me everywhere at once."

"That's right. And now I'm going to kiss you everywhere. Starting right here." She put her mouth under Beth's breast and licked her way up only to stop before she reached the rock-hard nipple. She changed direction and started licking around the areola, amazed at the way the dark pink skin puckered as Beth's chest heaved uncontrollably. "You want my lips right there, don't you?"

"Yes. Please Ciel."

CC obliged, closing her lips around the sensitive nipple and sucking it in, flicking her tongue over the tip. Beth moaned and pushed her breast deeper inside CC's mouth. CC stopped sucking but kept the nipple in her mouth when she asked, "Does it feel as good as you imagined?"

"Yes Ciel. You're everything I fantasized about and more. Please don't stop." CC went to Beth's other nipple and gave it the same kind of attention before she moved down to settle between Beth's legs and wrapped her arms around her thighs. She made herself comfortable; she planned on spending a lot of time there, the smell of Beth's desire intensifying her buzz.

Beth opened her legs wider and tipped her pelvis with anticipation. She was so ready for CC's mouth on her. CC saw it in her red, glistening lips and her swollen clitoris. She started caressing the dark, soft curls with her mouth, just a thin strip leading to parted lips.

Beth whimpered, waiting for the first touch of CC's tongue. When it finally came in one long stroke from her opening to her oversensitive bundle of nerves, she growled so loud and so deeply that CC felt it down to her own sex. She kept feasting on Beth in slow, thorough movements of her tongue and lips. She lapped up everything Beth had to give for a very, very long time, intoxicated with her smell and the sounds she made.

When Beth's thighs started trembling on either side of her face, communicating how close she was to orgasm, CC closed her mouth around her clitoris and penetrated her with two fingers. She sucked and fucked her just hard enough to bring her to climax, slow enough to make it last. Beth was loud, so surprisingly and beautifully loud. The sounds she made and the way she tightened around CC's fingers were enough for CC to come with her, albeit more discretely.

"That was so hot," CC said when she climbed back up next to Beth and kissed her.

Beth returned the kiss, clearly enjoying her own taste on CC's mouth. "So fucking hot." They lay on their backs, catching their breath, and CC smiled in complete satisfaction and serenity. She hadn't expected Beth to be this spontaneous, this sensual, this freaking amazing in bed. It was a surprise she cherished. Liz hadn't crossed her mind all night. *Until now.* The thought left her mind as quickly as it had come when Beth suddenly sat up straight in bed. "Do you have anything to eat? I'm starving."

CC laughed out loud and turned to Beth. "Of course. You can't smoke without being prepared for munchies. How does chocolate chunk ice cream sound?"

"Oh god, so fucking good. But we're so going to run tomorrow."

"This *is* tomorrow, sweetheart."

"Oh okay. We're going to run next tomorrow then."

"Okay, next tomorrow it is," CC agreed as she stood up and grabbed Beth's hand to lead her to the kitchen.

CHAPTER SEVENTEEN

CC ran next to Beth and Willow, grateful there was no snow on the ground. The cold of early January was making the run hard enough on her lungs without having to worry about slipping on ice. The snow that had fallen on Thanksgiving weekend and the few snowfalls after that hadn't stayed on the ground. What had remained since that first night they made love, however, were their mutual elation, desire and love. They rarely spent a night apart and CC reveled in the way their relationship grew stronger. They'd spent the Christmas holiday with Charles and Marie, and CC had gone to Buffalo to meet Beth's family on New Year's Eve. Charles and Marie instantly fell in love with Beth, and CC thought Beth's family liked her too.

Everything was going so well that she was tempted to simply delete the email that came from Liz shortly after they came back from Buffalo. Liz was going back to school in Albany and wanted to meet with CC to catch up. She said she wanted to apologize in person, and she hoped they could be friends. CC decided to talk about it with Beth. To her surprise Beth encouraged her to meet with Liz. CC was still not sure why. Dr. Simmons, whom CC had seen a few times, also thought meeting with Liz could be beneficial. Some kind of closure.

They hit the five-kilometer mark and started walking to cool down. "Are you sure you're okay with me having coffee with Liz this afternoon?"

Beth smiled at her. CC was still amazed at how fresh Beth could look after a five-kilometer run. She made it look easy while CC was red, sweaty and could hardly breathe. "I already told you, Ciel. I understand her need to apologize in person, and I surely think you deserve that apology."

"And that's why you're okay with it?" She saw Beth's nose wrinkle, which prompted her to add, "Or is there something else?"

Beth sighed deeply and took CC's hand. "Well, I guess if there's any chance you still have feelings for her I'd rather know about it now than later." Her voice was soft, adorably insecure. "Because I'm falling deeper in love with you every day, and if Liz is going to mess that up…"

"Shh." CC stopped Beth from taking her next step and turned to face her, quickly kissing her lips to keep her from finishing her sentence. "Liz doesn't have the power to mess anything up between us. If anything happened between Liz and me, I would be the one messing up the best thing that ever happened to me. I won't do that, Beth. I promise. I'm falling deeper every day too. For you. There's no going back now."

She ended with a smile in which she hoped Beth could read nothing but sincerity. They kissed again, slowly, as if they wanted to express all the depth of their love in one kiss. They broke the kiss when Willow whined her impatience from being still too long and they continued their walk back to the parking lot.

* * *

CC entered the Troy Daily Grind Café at five minutes before three. She ordered a latte and sat at a small table by the window. She was nervous. She meant her promise to Beth, but deep down she didn't know how seeing Liz again would affect her. How could she? She knew she wouldn't let anything she might feel interfere with her relationship with Beth, but it would be so much easier if there was no feeling at all to worry about. To have closure once and for all.

Liz entered the café five minutes after three. She smiled and waved at CC before getting in line to get her coffee, leaving CC with time to study her. Her red hair was shorter, barely touching her shoulders. Her emerald green eyes were sparkling, her full lips perfectly glossed. She looked healthy, and oh so gorgeous. That hadn't changed. CC felt her heart beat faster and the palms of her hands began to sweat. Her body had a raw physical attraction to that woman; she had no control over that.

Coffee in hand, Liz walked toward her table and smiled again. "Hi, thank you so much for coming."

"Hi," CC said timidly while Liz quickly set her coffee on the table and removed her winter jacket. She was wearing a green V neck sweater that made it difficult for CC not to look at her cleavage.

"Can I have a hug?"

"Sure," CC answered before she realized what she was saying. She stood up and let Liz pull her in a tight embrace that fortunately didn't last too long. CC sat back in her chair and Liz sat across from her.

They stared at each other awkwardly until Liz finally spoke. "So, how have you been? You look great. You've lost more weight, haven't you?"

"No, my weight has been stable for a while, but I'm still running so my body keeps changing."

"Well, either way you look hot," Liz concluded with a wink.

CC felt her cheeks blush profusely. "Thank you. And to answer your question I've been good, very good. You?"

"Much better. I'm still in therapy and probably will always be, but I'm well enough to go back to school and get on with my life."

"That's great, Liz. I'm very happy for you."

Another awkward silence followed during which they took a sip of their coffee and glanced out the window before looking at each other again. Liz lowered her eyes to her coffee, her well-manicured fingers playing with the rim of the cup. CC observed in silence, waiting for Liz to finally look up again and start talking.

"Okay, so I wanted to see you today to apologize again for the way I treated you. You didn't deserve that. You're such a good person, CC." She sounded edgy but sincere, more concerned with her message than with the way she delivered it. It was a nice change from the Liz she'd known.

"I appreciate the apology, Liz, especially since it seems really heartfelt."

"It is," she quickly emphasized. "Oh my god, CC, it's so totally heartfelt. There isn't a day that goes by that I don't think about how much I hurt you."

"I believe you." They drank their coffee in silence for a few minutes. Liz looked as though she hoped CC would say more. CC couldn't find anything else to say.

"There was another reason I wanted to see you today." CC nodded with apprehension. "I was hoping, well, since I'm back in Albany…" Liz hesitated, rambled, and CC suddenly felt anxious. She could no longer look at Liz in the eye and focused on the sweater she was wearing instead.

"See, I can't forget you, CC. I was hoping we could maybe start seeing each other once in a while and…" CC kept her eyes on the sweater and started fidgeting with the handle of her cup. "Well, we could see where that leads us." The green of Liz's sweater didn't match her eyes, CC noted. It was darker. It was closer to the color of Beth's eyes. "I guess what I'm asking for is a chance to prove myself to you, CC." Liz sighed, indicating she was done talking.

CC stared at the green of Beth's eyes on Liz's sweater and smiled before she replied.

"Liz, you're a wonderful woman. You're smart, talented and unbelievably gorgeous. The woman who is lucky enough to have your love, your real, beautiful, healthy love, will be a very fortunate woman. But that woman can't be me. Not now, not ever." Her voice was calm and determinate, leaving no room for hope.

"Why? You've met someone else?" Liz asked with a hint of a sneer.

"Yes, I have. But that's not the only reason why. Even if I didn't have that person in my life, I still couldn't be with you. That woman showed me the type of love I really want, the type of person I really want to be in a couple, and I know I couldn't have that or be that with you. I'm sorry." She finished her coffee and stood up to put on her jacket. "Thank you again for the apology, Liz. It means a lot to me. I honestly wish you nothing but the best. You really deserve it, no matter what you've done in the past. Don't forget that okay?"

"Okay," Liz said simply as she stared at her cup of coffee. CC put her hand on Liz's shoulder and squeezed it gently before walking out of the café. She couldn't help the smile on her face. She was free, completely free, and she needed to see Beth's eyes right away.

* * *

CC entered the small bungalow and Willow greeted her at the door. She got on her knees to pet the Boxer and then rose to take off her boots and jacket. She joined Beth in the kitchen, where she was busy cooking dinner. "What are we having?" CC asked.

"Pasta. Garlic and oil sauce."

CC walked behind Beth and placed a light kiss on the back of her neck. "Yummy. What can I do to help?"

Beth turned to kiss CC on the lips and went back to her sauce. "You can start on the salad. I got all the veggies out of the fridge already." They cooked together in silence for a few minutes before Beth asked, "So, are you going to tell me how it went?" Her question was loaded with dread.

"It went very well," CC offered. "Her apology seemed sincere. And then she said she wanted me to give her another chance."

"Oh?" Beth turned to CC. Her face was marked with fear. "And what did you say?"

CC smiled and put her arms around Beth's waist. The warm embrace comforted Beth, and CC felt her relax in her arms even before she answered her question. "I told her I couldn't do that."

Beth smiled and placed her own arms on CC's shoulders. "You did, huh? So, no residual feelings in here?" she asked, gently tapping CC's chest.

"Well, she's still hot," CC admitted mockingly with a mischievous grin.

Beth hit her shoulder lightly even as she laughed. "You ass," she said playfully.

"Wait, you didn't let me finish."

"All right, I'm listening. You better make it good."

"Liz is gorgeous, but it doesn't matter. There was only one woman in my mind and in my heart when I was with her. You. Even her green sweater reminded me of your eyes and when I left that café I couldn't get here quick enough. I just wanted to be with you. Is that better?"

Beth smiled and her eyes welled up with tears. "Much, much better. But what would make it even better is if you kissed me like you mean it. Right now."

CC giggled before she obliged and kissed Beth. She took her time exploring her lover's mouth. This kiss was more than a kiss. It was a promise, a commitment, a forever.

Bella Books, Inc.

Women. Books. Even Better Together.

P.O. Box 10543
Tallahassee, FL 32302

Phone: 800-729-4992
www.bellabooks.com